THE RISK TAKER

BOSTON HAWKS HOCKEY
BOOK 2

GINA AZZI

THREE CITIES PUBLISHING LLC

The Risk Taker

Copyright © 2021 by Gina Azzi

All rights reserved.

No part of this publication may be reproduced, distributed, or transmitted in any form or by any means, including photocopying, recording, or other electronic or mechanical methods, without the prior written permission of the publisher, except in the case of brief quotations embodied in critical reviews and certain other noncommercial uses permitted by copyright law.

This is a work of fiction. Names, characters, businesses, places, events, locales, and incidents are either the products of the author's imagination or used in a fictitious manner. Any resemblance to actual persons, living or dead, or actual events is purely coincidental.

ISBN: 978-1-968159-13-9

CHAPTER 1
EASTON

I hate that she's here.

I hate that she's staring at me like she doesn't know me anymore. Her eyes, a brilliant shade of blue, are too wide in her face. Her mouth, luscious lips I've dreamt of tasting, are pressed tightly together.

Of all the people I'd hate to see me leaving rehab, Claire Merrick is at the top of my list. She's my best friend's little sister and has been affectionately adopted as such by all the guys on my hockey team.

I've known Claire since she was a seven-year-old brat with pigtails and a crooked smile, but somewhere over the years, she became a hell of a lot more than just Austin's kid sister. Not that I'd ever let her know that.

Not that I want anyone to know that. Especially not now that I'm a washed-up NHL player completing my second stint in rehab in two years.

Moments ago, Claire's parents, Mary and Joe, welcomed me back with their open arms and accepting smiles. They are more of parents to me than my own, and disappointing them aches almost as much as seeing the hurt in Claire's eyes.

Damn it. This isn't what I need right now.

Claire steps out more from behind Austin and my eyes drop to the curves of her frame. Jesus, she's beautiful. Too fucking innocent and sweet to be standing inside of a rehab center. She flips her hair over her shoulder, her fingers playing with the ends nervously.

I narrow my eyes. Why is she here? How many people do I have to disappoint today by being the asshole who got tossed in rehab for a second time, practically ruining my career?

Claire drops her eyes to the ground and I look away.

"You look good, East." My brother clasps his hand on my shoulder before pulling me into a man hug. "Happy you're home."

"Thanks, Noah." I smack my brother's back before turning to his girl who I haven't seen in ages. I mean, I saw her a handful of months ago but I haven't really spoken to her in years. "Hey Indy."

She smiles softly, wrapping her arms around my waist. "Good to see you, Easton."

I wrap my arm around her and don't miss the way my brother's eyes widen, filled with happiness at seeing me get along with his girl. His pregnant girl who he wants to wifey. Damn. Witnessing Noah be so open with his emotions hits me with a pang. He's healing, moving forward with his life, on from our parents' bullshit. Yet I'm still struggling, barely keeping my head above water. In this moment, the differences between us are staggering.

Indy slips away and begins to shrug into her coat, my brother quick to help her.

Austin shakes my hand and bangs his fist against my shoulder, grinning at me. "Team's missed you."

I nod and chuckle, the feeling in my chest giving way to a blaze of panic.

The team. Do they even want me back after how every-thing went down? Aren't they going to keep the new guy Sims playing in my position? At least Sims is reliable, dependable; he shows up.

"No pressure but we'd love to have you back at prac-tice whenever you're ready."

I nod, clearing my throat. "Hell yeah, man. Can't wait to get back on the ice." It's the truth; I really can't wait to get back on the ice. But it's not the full truth. Because then I'd have to admit that I'm petrified to get back on the ice in front of thousands of people and listen to all their jeers and taunts and fuck, my stomach feels sick, I don't know if I'm ready for it. I sure as hell don't feel ready for anything right now, but everyone expects me to be better.

Healed. Recovered. Whole. So that's what I'll try to be. Better.

I turn my attention to Claire. She offers me a small wave and an unsteady smile. It pisses me off the second I see it because there's nothing unsure about Claire. The girl oozes confidence, calls people out on their bullshit, and never seems hesitant, the way she is right now. "What are you doing here?" I ask.

She stiffens at my tone and I hear the inhale she sucks in. Her eyes narrow and a thrill shoots through me. There she is. "Came to see you."

"Why?" I scrub my hand over my forehead, my fingers swiping over the scar that cuts through my eyebrow like a warning. A reminder.

She crosses her arms, staring at me. "Because I'm not a dick." She pushes past me and I snicker, keeping my back to her.

If only Claire knew how much she gets under my skin.

If she had any idea how much I feel for her, how much I crave her, she wouldn't understand why I've spent years of my life keeping her at arm's length.

But it's for the best.

Claire is Austin's little sister.

She's larger than life, outgoing, and authentic.

The last thing she needs is an alcoholic who keeps falling off the wagon.

After all, it's only a matter of time 'til I'm back here. With so many people on my list to let down and disappoint, I can't afford to add another.

I catch the way Indy's lips purse and how she slips from Noah's grasp to trail after her cousin. My brother shoots me a confused look but I ignore it. The truth is, I've busted Claire's balls for years. The only reason why my brother cares now is because his girl seems affected by it.

Sighing, I tilt my head toward the parking lot. "You guys want to get out of here?"

"Yeah." Austin clasps my shoulder. "Let's go grab a bite. What are you in the mood for?"

My mouth waters just thinking of all the amazing food I've missed out on. "Mexican."

Noah grins. "I know just the place. It's close to Indy's apartment. It's Mexican fusion with some flair. I think you'll like it."

I snort, lifting an eyebrow at Noah. "Mexican fusion with flair? Where did my growly brother who only eats sandwiches go?"

Austin chuckles. "See what I mean?" He points to Noah. "Noah's a whole new man now. My cousin elevated his tastes."

I snicker but Noah lets our ribbing roll off his back.

"I swear it's really good. Torsten introduced me to the

restaurant," he continues, mentioning one of the defenseman on our team who is a massive foodie.

"All right, let's try it," I agree. I don't really care where we go—or what we eat—as long as I can kick it with my brother and best friend and regain a little social normalcy.

When we push into the cold air, I close my eyes and breathe in. It's sunny today but crisp and cold. The kind of cold that makes your breath escape your mouth in little white clouds but turns the sky bright blue. I stride beside Austin as Noah leads us to the cars.

Mary and Joe are already sitting inside theirs with the heat blasting. Mary waves again when she sees me and I can't help but smile at the woman I probably love most in the world. I know I shouldn't admit that since I have a real mom but Mary Merrick is worth ten Debra Scotch's if you know what I'm saying.

Mary rolls down the window of her car and holds out a Starbucks cup. "Here, Easton."

I take the cup and shake my head when I read the white sticker label. "You brought me hot chocolate?"

"It's your favorite." She shrugs. "With whipped cream."

"How'd you even remember that?"

Mary grins, tipping her head toward Claire who stands next to the driver's side window, chatting with Indy. "Claire did. She thought you'd want something warm on such a cold day. And something that would make you smile."

I do. Smile, I mean. I raise my cup toward Mary and Joe and say, "Thank you," even though my eyes are trained on Claire.

Something feels strange in my chest as I process that Claire did something thoughtful for me. Hell she showed up today, and I immediately pissed her off.

I take a gulp of the hot chocolate, closing my eyes as I savor the taste.

Claire's always been extra like that. Always going out of her way to do something kind for someone—one of the guys on the team, her best friend Rielle, her cousin Indy—if she thinks they need a pick-me-up. The weird thing is, she never wants credit for it. It's as if seeing that person smile is all the thanks she needs.

I both revel in and despise the fact that she would do something thoughtful, even if it's small and simple, for me. Because I've rarely, if ever, been considerate of her.

"Okay, let's head out. Mom and Dad, we're going to grab a bite at that Mexican spot near Indy's if you want to come?" Austin bumps my shoulder as he leans down to talk to his parents through the car window.

"That's okay, guys. You go and enjoy," I hear Joe say.

"We can set things up at home for Easton?" Mary asks, her voice softer.

"Nah, I think Noah's got everything ready," Austin replies. "I'm going to toss East's bag in the other car." He butts his fist against the roof of the car as he says goodbye to his parents.

I swallow against the tightness in my throat. I hate that so many people have gone out of their way to make my transition smoother. I hate that I am essentially a big man-child who still needs babysitting. Someone to make sure the house is emptied of liquor. Someone to make sure my room is cleaned and my bed freshly laundered. Jesus, when will I stop being such a fuckup and start manning up?

"Thanks again for coming. It means a lot." I wave to Mary and Joe as Joe puts the car in reverse and begins to back out of the spot.

As their car pulls away, Indy smirks. "Think we can all fit in one ride?"

Austin groans as he closes the trunk of a small Honda Civic.

"Whose car is this?" I ask.

"Mine." Indy raises her hand.

"You're not sitting in the back." Noah points at her.

She rolls her eyes, muttering to Claire. "You get pregnant and suddenly you're an invalid. Can't even sit in the back seat."

Claire smirks. "I don't know why you're complaining. Now you can ride up front with me." She takes a set of car keys from Indy's hand and dangles them.

Austin snatches them from her grasp. "No way. The three of us won't even fit back there." He tosses the keys to Noah. "East and I will sit in the back. Claire's so tiny she can fit anywhere."

Claire's cheeks redden and she shoots me a surreptitious glance, her eyes darting away as soon as she catches me looking at her. I take another sip of my hot chocolate before Noah swipes it from my hand and slides behind the wheel. He places the cup in a cup holder and I fight the urge to laugh. Indy sits in the passenger seat and Austin climbs into the back.

I hold the door open for Claire. "After you." My voice is lower than it was in the rehab center, less biting.

She shoots me a look I can't decipher over her shoulder. For a breath, it's like she can see through me, all the way down to the dark thoughts I keep hidden. Then she sighs and slides into the car.

I get in after her and shift my weight, trying to get comfortable. Claire is completely squished between her brother and me, contorting her body to balance her weight on her hip.

Noah turns on the car and a Meghan Trainor song blares from the speakers. He chuckles, Indy sings along, and Claire grins, not even embarrassed when her brother starts making fun of her and Indy for their shitty taste in music.

"You know you secretly listen," she tells Austin. "How else could you have gotten any dates in high school if it wasn't for your snooping whenever Vanny and I had girl talk?"

Indy laughs and asks a question about Claire and Austin's older sister Savannah. But I stop paying attention because Noah breaks hard at a stop sign and Claire's body swings toward mine, her ample cleavage nearly in my face.

She flushes as she grips the back of the passenger seat, trying to steady herself. Her breathing ticks up, her chest heaving, and I can't tear my eyes away. Shit. I force myself to glance up and her blue eyes latch onto mine, swirling and complicated. For a breath, the tension between us swells like a thundercloud and my skin tingles.

Swearing, I wrap my arm around her waist and tug her into my lap. My other hand clamps down on top of her knee to keep her steady as Noah makes a turn.

"You okay?" I murmur.

She wiggles her ass against my lap and I swallow against the swear I want to let loose. Because just feeling Claire rub up against me has my thoughts running and my body reacting. My hand grips her knee tighter and her wiggling stops. Instead, she sits ramrod straight and nods. "I'm fine."

CHAPTER 2
CLAIRE

"I can't believe you've never taken me here," I scold my cousin Indy as we step into the little Mexican restaurant she frequents.

Indy shrugs. "I usually come to your house."

"We need to change that. My parents are driving me insane." I wrinkle my nose.

"Still no luck with the job search?" Indy asks, tipping her head in the direction of a table.

I trail her. "Nothing permanent. Still just freelancing. Although the last job I did should lead to some more work."

"You're an amazing graphic designer, Claire. You *will* find something."

"Nothing that will let me get out from under my parents' roof," I mutter, instantly swelling with chagrin. It's not that I'm *not* thankful to Mom and Dad, because I am. It's just that they still treat me like I'm in high school, and after four years of being away at university, it's been hard to fall back in line when I'd rather do my own thing.

Indy shoots me a sympathetic look as we sit down at a table in the back.

Noah passes out the menus. For a few moments, it's silent. Stifled. Everyone studies their menu but it's more than that. No one knows what to say, how to act, now that Easton is here, sitting with us. A lot has changed in the past ninety days. For starters, Noah hooked up with Indy and got her pregnant. Eddie Sims has taken over Easton's position on the Boston Hawks as the starting left winger. And, I'm still living at home. So I guess nothing major has happened in my life, but for some reason, things between Easton and me feel different now too.

Gone is the easygoing sibling-like teasing he used to spit my way. Instead, he glares now, calling me "kid" with an edge instead of as an endearment. We've barely spoken since he left rehab the first time, a year ago now, and while my torch for him continues to burn, he glowers at me like he doesn't understand why I'm here.

I pinch the menu tighter between my fingertips, feeling my shoulders tense as I duck my head. I've never been shy around guys. I grew up around way too many of them as Savannah and Austin's little sister. But Easton Scotch has always caused me to grow tongue-tied and giggly. Another thing I dislike.

"Hey guys. My name is Shell and I'll be taking care of you today." Our server stops at the end of the table and all eyes swing toward her. "Can I get you started with drinks?"

Austin opens his mouth and snaps it closed again. Noah and Indy exchange a look. Easton swears. "For fuck's sake, get a beer or a margarita or whatever. I'm fine. Really."

I sigh. "I'll take a Diet Coke please. On the rocks, with a twist of lemon."

Shell grins but I feel the death glare Easton pierces my cheek with. The rest of the table orders drinks and Noah tacks on a bunch of appetizers to start. As soon as Shell is out of sight, Noah sighs and leans back in his chair.

Easton glances at his brother. "You okay? Noah, I swear, I'm good."

"I know, East. It's not that. It's just, well…"

Indy leans forward and Easton's eyes dart from his brother to Indy and back again.

"It's just that with Indy being pregnant, things have changed," Noah says without saying anything at all.

Austin bites his lip, trying to stifle his laughter.

"No shit, man. I'm about to be an uncle." East laughs.

Noah works a swallow, glancing at Indy for moral support. "I'm planning on moving in with Indy. Permanently. We're having a baby and—"

Easton frowns, holding up his hand. "Of course you're moving in with Indy. I didn't expect you not to."

Relief filters through Noah's eyes as some of the tension in his shoulders leaks away. "Really?"

"Of course. No offense but I've lived on my own before. You know when you and—"

"Right, I know," Noah cuts him off before Easton can mention Noah's ex-fiancée Courtney.

The stifling silence hovers over the table once more. Because Courtney is not the only thing that's not being mentioned. What no one wants to say is that when East did live on his own, his alcoholism veered from *functioning* to *destructive*.

Austin clears his throat and East's head swivels toward my brother. Something passes between them and Easton's head drops, a snort sounding from his nose. "Right. But when Noah lived with Courtney, I fucked up my whole life."

"That's not what I—" Noah starts but Easton shakes his head.

"It's fine, Noah. Honestly, I get it. You're about to become a father. I don't expect you to miss out on a second of Indy's pregnancy. I don't want you to stop living your life so you can hold my hand." He shoots a sad smile to Indy before turning back to his brother. "I swear, my head is on straight this time. I'm *fine*."

"Mom and Dad offered for you to move in with them," Austin announces as Shell drops off our drinks.

Say what? My attention snaps to Austin as a wave of panic rolls through my body. My eyes widen in alarm. He wants Easton to live under my parents' roof? In our family home? With me only two doors down from the guest bedroom? I pick up my Diet Coke and take a large gulp, suddenly wishing it was straight tequila.

"Or," Indy says slowly, her eyes darting around the table, "Claire can move in with you."

I sputter on the Diet Coke. Did I hear that wrong? I must have heard her wrong.

Because, what the hell is going on? What is everyone thinking? And why didn't I know any of their thoughts?

"What?" Noah chuckles.

"No fucking way," Easton spits.

"Why would Claire do that?" Austin asks.

Once again, Shell has impeccable timing and delivers some appetizers. I stuff a nacho piled with sushi into my mouth, too panicked to fully appreciate the fusion element of this restaurant, and buy myself some time before I murder my cousin in a sea of pico de gallo and sriracha.

"No, think about it," Indy continues calmly. "Everyone, maybe even you"—she smiles at Easton—"would feel better if you weren't living solo. Claire's desperate to get out of living with Aunt Mary and Uncle Joe. Your place is spacious enough. Your paths won't cross unless you want them to. But Claire can be an extra support person and y'all would be doing her a massive favor too." Indy smirks at me, shooting me a wink.

I choke on my nacho and reach for my Diet Coke again. I need something to do with my hands so I don't reach for Indy. I need something to do with my mouth so I don't word vomit really bad words onto the table.

Noah is silent for a second before he looks at his brother. "It isn't a *bad* idea."

I take a long gulp.

Austin furrows his brow. "You want out of Mom and Dad's house that badly?"

I feel Easton's gaze again but I don't turn to make eye contact. Is he curious about my response because of how it affects him? Or is he actually interested in my life?

I clear my throat and nod. "Look, Mom and Dad are the best. But I'm going to be twenty-five, Aus. They're still trying to saddle me with a curfew and call me whenever I take a Lyft or Uber to make sure I've properly identified the driver." I cut a quick look at Easton. His mouth is thin, his eyes narrowed, his face giving away none of the thoughts I know are turning over in his mind. "I've been trying to save. I was going to talk to Torsten about those rentals he owns on the Waterfront. Maybe—"

"No." The sound of Easton's voice, cold and hard and decisive, cuts me off.

"What?" I ask him.

"You're not living in fucking Southie, Claire. Not that Joe would ever allow it."

"Once again, I'm going to be twenty-five," I remind him, my tone clipped. My dad can tell me what to do under his roof but not out in the real world where I'm a real adult.

Austin shakes his head, no doubt against my living on the Waterfront. It's hardly South Boston anymore, with the way the area has been redeveloped. In fact, I doubt I could afford an apartment in any of the buildings Torsten owns. But my best friend Rielle lives a handful of streets over from the Waterfront and she's had several *interesting* encounters. Austin opens his mouth, most likely to echo Easton when East shifts in his chair. "Move in," he demands harshly, surprising everyone at the table, especially me.

I look at him, noting the challenge that sparks in his blue eyes. Is he serious right now?

"Two birds, one stone," Indy adds like her plan is the most brilliant idea ever.

"I'll talk to Mom and Dad," Austin offers. "I'm sure they'll have some reservations but honestly, Claire, I'd feel a hell of a lot better if you were in Beacon Hill with East than living solo on the Waterfront."

"Rielle lives in Southie and she's fine."

Austin's expression tightens. "Dad's not going to buy that."

I sigh, knowing he's right, and look at Noah. Then Easton. "I can pay you rent."

Noah waves his hand. "No way. You can look out for my brother and save your money."

"Are you sure?" I ask.

"He's sure," Easton tacks on. His expression is fierce when it meets mine. A tight jaw, a slight curl to his upper lip, but his eyes, gah, they pierce my soul. Hot and angry, intense and pleading. "But just because we're going to be roommates doesn't mean I need you all up in my business. In my life. I don't need a babysitter."

I hold up my hands, settling back in my seat. "Got it. Same goes for you. I have my own life." I smile sweetly.

Easton's eyes narrow further as he glares at me. I have no clue what he hopes to find, but dissatisfied, he finally turns away.

I kick Indy under the table and she grins, truly believing that she made the romantic match of the century. Jeez, nothing could be further from the truth.

I may still get giddy and tongue-tied around Easton and his deep blue eyes, full mouth, and body like a freaking underwear model, but that doesn't mean I want to babysit him either.

I don't want to see the women he brings home late at night. Or the ones who walk out of his bedroom door with their perky breasts and perfect morning hair. I don't want to be mesmerized by the ink that crawls up his ribcage or spans his shoulder blades. And I certainly don't want to lie in bed at night thinking of him, naked, just down the hall.

But my body doesn't care about logic or self-preservation. A thrill shimmies down my spine at the thought of being so close to him. My heart beats faster at the realization that it will just be the two of us. Alone.

I can pretend all I want but living with Easton Scotch is far from a hardship. Will we become friends again? Will he talk to me about real things the way he used to?

I hide my smile by biting into a chip. At the very least, rent-free living away from Mom and Dad is a total win.

CHAPTER 3
EASTON

S he shows up in a blaze of pink.

With a polka dot duffle bag on her shoulder and a rose-colored rolling suitcase, Claire appears on my front porch. Her blonde curls bounce, and when she smiles, I taste bubble gum. Jesus, she looks like Reese Witherspoon from *Legally Blonde*. Clueless but with her heart in the right place.

I roll my eyes and turn my back after she clears the threshold of my Beacon Hill brownstone.

Claire follows me into the kitchen, drops her baggage, and slides onto a barstool.

I sigh, turning toward her. "You sure about this?"

"I'd pretty much do anything to not live with my parents," she admits.

I raise an eyebrow.

Her cheeks pinken and she looks like her luggage. "Well, not *anything*."

I scowl, hating the innuendo she casually tossed out.

Claire tilts her head. "But I'd live with you," she adds sweetly.

I snort and fill up two glasses of water. I slide one across the island to her and she wraps her hands around it, staring down at its contents before lifting her gaze to meet mine.

I stare back, not offering anything as the tension between us intensifies from a gentle breeze to a gust of wind. It's always been this way with Claire. Well, not always, but definitely for the past five years. That's why I keep her at arm's length. That's why I try to limit my one-on-one interactions with her.

And now, she's my roomie.

And I'm sober. Shit. I chuckle, shaking my head.

Claire's eyes narrow. "Look, I get that you don't want me here and it's cool. I swear I'm not trying to step on your toes or cramp your style or whatever you think I'm doing. I just need some space from my parents, some… room to figure out what I'm doing with my life. And even if you don't believe me, I hate the thought of you being on your own during all of this." She gestures at me as if my standing in my kitchen encompasses all the bullshit that goes along with being a recovering alcoholic.

Still, her words pierce my chest because as much as I don't want to want her, a thrill zips through me that she thinks of me. That she *cares*. Damn it. I squeeze the bridge of my nose, pinching the inner corners of my eyes. For years, I did this to try to clear my head.

But for the first time in a long time, my head is clear. Crystal. And the overwhelming realization that Claire Merrick is too good, too young, too *complicated* for me slaps me hard in the face.

She's my best friend's little sister. She is the actual daughter of the people I wish were my parents. She's twenty-four, doesn't have a steady job, and up until an hour ago, still lived with her mom and dad.

I look her over, note the blush high on her cheeks, the worry mixed with strength in her eyes, the way she hasn't touched her water. I look her over searching for a real flaw, something I can latch onto, but instead, I want to pull her across the island and kiss her. Hard.

I sigh. "Whatever, Claire. I don't care one way or the other if you're here. I have no intention of going out and partying or staying in and getting wasted solo. Noah's already searched every inch of this house and there's no booze to be had. I don't need a babysitter, hell, I don't even need a friend. But if you need a place to blow off steam, or find yourself, have at it." I lift my chin toward the stairs. "Guest room is the first door on the left." I stride past the refrigerator, slapping it with my palm. "Help yourself to whatever."

I move to exit the room but Claire's voice stops me in my tracks.

"Uh, I need a favor."

I stop walking, keeping my back turned to her. Of course she does. Why the hell did anyone think this would be a good idea? I feel her gaze on my back and my shoulders stiffen under her perusal.

"What is it?" I ask, my tone clipped.

"Part of my parents agreeing to my moving in here is that we go to their house for Sunday night family dinners."

I whip around. "We?"

She nods, offering a small smile. "I told them you'd love to."

Is she kidding me? Look, I love Mary and Joe but that doesn't mean I want to sit around their harvest table with their perfect offspring every Sunday and pretend I'm not the biggest screwup in the room. "Without asking me first?"

She rolls her eyes, giving me that attitude I crave. "What's the big deal, Scotch? It's not like you to pass up a homecooked meal."

I blow out a breath, shaking my head. I hate that she's right but I do love Mary's cooking. "Whatever, Merrick. Just don't make this a habit." I gesture between us.

"This?" She cocks her head, her eyes taunting, her lips pursed.

Sweet Jesus, why does this girl get under my skin? "Yeah, making decisions for us. Like we're some kind of a package deal. I get that we're now technically roommates but that's as far as this goes. You do you and I'll do me."

She stares at me hard. "Got it, boss."

"See ya around, Claire." I leave the kitchen and collect her suitcase and duffle bag.

My blood is pumping too fast in my veins as I take the stairs two at a time.

What the hell was my brother thinking? I've been out of rehab for five minutes and I've got a new roommate, a career hanging by a thread, and a weekly dinner commitment.

I shake my head and drop Claire's belongings in the guest bedroom. Then, I push into my bedroom and kick the door closed behind me. My hands clench into fists and a desire to find a bottle and gulp it scrapes my throat raw.

Three months ago, I thought I'd never survive rehab.

Now, I wonder if I'll survive Claire.

WHEN I WALK DOWNSTAIRS to the game room Noah and I always hung around in, I do a double take.

Christ, for a blink, I forgot Claire would be here. And not just here, in my house, but here, in all of my space.

She shifts on the large wraparound sofa when she sees me. "Hey." Her voice is flat and she goes back to polishing her toenails some hot pink color I can't tear my gaze from.

In the background, a reality TV show flickers across the big screen TV, shrill voices and empty threats. "You watch this shit?"

"It's entertaining."

I kick back on the couch beside her, raising my feet to the ottoman. "What have you got going on this week?"

She glances at me from the corner of her eye, her expression tight. For the first time, I notice how tense she looks. It bothers me because Claire has always been so chill around me. Growing up with her means I've already seen her at her worst, a thousand times over, so for her to be unsure around me now is…unsettling.

"Oh, I don't know," she sighs. "Probably send out a new batch of resumes to companies I'll most likely never hear back from. Not even a generic rejection." She twists the cap on her nail polish and leans back against the couch cushion, placing her feet on the other side of the ottoman. She rolls her head to face me. "This economy sucks but even if it didn't, I'm not really qualified for much."

"What are you talking about? You've got your degree."

She snorts. "In graphic design." Her eyes close and I sense the defeat she doesn't want me to see. "I graduated in May, East. That was more than six months ago, and other than a handful of freelancing jobs I've found online, I don't have much to show for it. If it wasn't for Derek and his band, I wouldn't have had a paying gig for the past two months."

Derek? At the mention of a guy I don't know, I sit up a little straighter. Is she dating someone? Does she have a boyfriend? A boyfriend who's in a freaking band? I clear my throat. "Derek?"

She waves a hand dismissively. "Just a guy I know. I did some work for his band over the summer and he's hooked me up with some other indie artists. Thank God for that as they're the only clients I currently have."

"What kind of work?" I know I'm overthinking it. I must be because Claire didn't mention Derek's name the way she would if they were involved. But, *still*. Musicians have a lot of the same stereotypes as professional athletes. And I'm too familiar with all of them.

"Logo design and branding. Merchandise. A few album covers. That kind of thing."

I stare at her for a long beat, seeing the frustration in her eyes. I heave out a sigh. "Listen, kid, you're being too hard on yourself." I shake my head. "I'm a washed-up hockey player who hit my prime about three years ago." I quirk an eyebrow as she scowls. "I just got out of rehab, Claire. You think I don't get feeling useless?"

"It's not the same thing."

"Really?"

She sits up straighter, her eyes flashing. "You *are* successful, Easton. You're an NHL player who can afford your own living space." She flaps her arms out to encompass the sick game room Noah and I decorated years ago. It was the first space in the house we designed. "And yeah, you went to rehab. But you completed it. You owned up to your mistakes, confronted your demons, and came out the other side." Her gaze intensifies, blue fire. "We're nothing alike." Her tone is soft when she says it and I can tell it's not a dig at me, but at herself.

Something in my chest shifts. I hear the defensiveness in her voice when she makes excuses for me. It's a grace she doesn't have for herself and it frustrates me. Claire is fifteen times more the person than I'll ever be. And she's wrong, I haven't owned shit. My demons haunt me every damn night and they're a hell of a lot uglier than a lack of job prospects. I rub the pad of my finger over the scar in my eyebrow.

I cluck my tongue at her. "You're right."

A flare of pain blooms in her eyes. Damn it, she took my words the wrong way. Of course she did. I never get anything right when it comes to Claire. *So why the hell are you still trying?*

Hurt wraps around her as she folds into herself and focuses hard on the TV personalities.

"Claire," I sigh, wanting her to know I meant that she's so much better, more than, me.

"Forget it, East."

"Aw, come on, kid—"

She stands from the couch and tosses me the remote control. "I've got some cover letters to write anyway." Clasping her nail polish tight in her fist, she leaves me alone in the game room.

I listen to her footsteps on the stairs and hate myself for making her feel more uncertain when that was never my intention. The truth is, Claire Merrick tempts me in ways she shouldn't.

She's both an angel and a devil. Sweet and innocent. Young and careful. And strong and fierce, wild and bold. I've wanted to taste her lips and thread my fingers through her hair for years now. Since the night of her twentieth birthday party when I looked at her, dancing with her arms in the air, a slinky gold dress riding up her thighs, and realized the girl I've always gone out of my way to protect turned into a woman. A woman I have no business fantasizing about. A woman who needs protection from guys *like* me.

I rub the heel of my hand against the center of my chest. I hate that she misinterpreted my words. I hate that I hurt her feelings when I spent years checking the immature guys in her class for teasing her about anything.

But isn't it better this way?

Claire will never be mine. She's not meant for a guy like me and I will never be good enough for her.

CHAPTER 4
CLAIRE

"What's it like living with him?" Indy stage-whispers as Noah bangs around in the upstairs bathroom.

"Is he searching for alcohol?" I lift an eyebrow at my cousin.

Her cheeks burn as she plops down on a barstool and nods toward the muffins I made on the kitchen island. "Are you baking for him?" Her eyes gleam.

"Indiana."

Indy sighs. "Look, Austin's just worried, okay?"

"He can't go snooping through his brother's things."

"Like you haven't already?" She calls me out and I flip her the middle finger. Indy laughs. "Trust me, I get it. Everyone is just worried about him. No one thinks he's going to go buy a six-pack, but if he happens to come across some liquor and it's a trigger and…"

"Didn't Noah already do a sweep before Easton left rehab?" I ask, setting a muffin on a plate and sliding it in front of her.

"Blueberry! Oh my God, I am having all the fruit cravings." She picks up the muffin and eyes it appreciatively. Flicking her gaze to me, she nods. "He did. But he forgot the guest—your—bathroom. Besides, he also wants to pack up some things to bring to my place."

"I can't believe you guys are living in that tiny shoebox." I laugh, popping a decaf Nespresso pod into the machine for her.

"I know." She grins. "But honestly, I love my little tenement apartment. I don't know if it will be practical for when the baby comes, but for right now, with Noah and I still getting to know each other and everything just so... new, moving would be too much stress."

"I know what you mean." I plunk down her mug and she gasps.

"Muffin and caffeine? I am so your favorite girl cousin."

"You're my only girl cousin," I remind her, snagging a muffin for myself and leaning over the kitchen island. "And don't get too excited. It's decaf."

Indy wrinkles her nose. She takes a big bite of her muffin and groans appreciatively.

"Good, right?"

"The best, Claire. If you don't land a job soon, you could give baking a shot."

I roll my eyes. "Just eat your muffin."

Indy takes another bite. "Where is East anyway?"

"AA meeting."

"Is he going every day?"

"Sometimes twice a day."

"Wow. I'm really proud of him," Indy says softly, a thoughtful look crossing her face.

"Yeah, me too."

"Has it been...okay, living with him?"

"It's been fine."

Indy's eyes narrow. "Just fine? Claire, you have pined for Easton since—"

"Shh!"

We both stop talking as we listen for Noah upstairs. After a moment, he drops something and groans loudly.

"I didn't pine," I begin but Indy's snort cuts me off. "It's just, it's different now. We used to at least be friends. This Easton looks at me like he can't stand me. He's constantly calling me kid. *Kid*, Indy, like I'm a preteen with a crush. It's annoying. And embarrassing because it's true." I stuff a huge bite of muffin in my mouth to stop the word vomit spewing from my lips.

I hate that Easton hurt my feelings but he did. For a second, just a blink, when he came into the game room, I thought we might hang out. Have a conversation, watch some TV, you know, be casual. Normal. But then he reminded me how different we are. How I'm an immature, bratty kid and he's a hockey god, and the disparity between us scraped at my insecurities. For the most part, I keep them buried so deep that most people don't think I have them. To the world, I project confidence, but sometimes, it's flimsy.

I know I'm a great flirt. I'm fun and outgoing. I have no problem talking to anyone.

But Easton makes me feel off-balanced and the other night, it's like he shoved me until I toppled over. With my lack of job prospects and my lack of a dating life, the high I've been riding since college graduation has been steadily shrinking as reality sets in.

Indy shoots me a sympathetic glance. "Claire, you told me that you and Easton always had a playful relationship. I'm sure he doesn't mean anything by it."

I shake my head. "It's different now. It just feels…off."

"Well, you both have a lot going on."

"Him more than me." I pick at my muffin.

"Don't blow off your stuff. Graduating and trying to find your footing after college is tough."

"I just wish I had a real job. With a salary," I sigh.

"You will. I swear." She holds up a hand before I can say anything. "And before you start, I know I wasn't in the same boat. I know I lucked out with my position at Brighton University. But Claire, when you find a job, you're going to be working for the next forty or fifty years. I know it doesn't seem like it but in the grand scheme of things, having eight or ten or even fourteen months of job searching isn't going to be the end of the world. I mean, look at you, living in this beautiful space with a boy you adore." She grins at me. "Take this time to hone your skills, cast a wide net for job prospects. Don't be so hard on yourself." She takes a sip of her coffee, her eyes meeting mine over the rim.

"I've been designing band logos and album covers for fun," I blurt out.

"Album covers?" Surprise layers her tone but she leans closer in interest. "Because of the thing with Derek?"

I roll my eyes. Hooking up with Derek over the summer was an awful decision. Sure, he's hot and reckless, wild and uninhibited. When he croons onstage, women scream his name, and I'm embarrassed to admit I was one of them. But after a whirlwind few weeks with high highs and low lows, I ended up a little emotionally bruised and financially broke.

"Yeah. He introduced me to some other indie bands, mostly local, who are looking for design work for covers, logos, and merchandise."

"I didn't realize you guys were talking again." Indy's voice is stiff, her eyes searching mine. Her disapproval is obvious and it makes me want to hug her and thank her for always having my back.

"We're not," I assure her.

She breathes out a sigh of relief. "Thank God. The way he stuck you with that bill at Carters Steakhouse was—"

"Shitty."

"And shady."

The night that Derek and his band, The Burnt Clovers, were invited to go on tour as the opening act for The Failed Poets, we all went to Carters, a super swanky downtown steakhouse that costs a small fortune, to celebrate. I had been drinking all night, cheering on my man, and was already quite drunk before I lifted a menu. I was definitely too tipsy to question how he secured a reservation last minute.

By the time dessert came, most of the band members and their significant others had bounced. Taylor, the drummer, had given me a sympathetic look as he kissed my cheek goodbye. "Want me to walk you out?" he offered. But I shook my head, gesturing to Derek and Callie, a girl he'd been friends with for years, still sitting at the table. A few minutes later, Callie whispered something to Derek and he nodded, giving me a long look. He told me they'd be back in a minute and I assumed they were going to smoke up or do a line of coke or some other shit I had no interest in.

I assumed wrong. Because I ended up paying a $3200 bill that effectively wiped out my tiny savings account. Then, I found Derek banging Callie in the alleyway I cut through to meet my Uber driver. It was an awful, humiliating night. And the reality check I desperately needed to wake the hell up and think seriously about my life choices.

"When did he reach out to you?" Indy asks, pulling me back to our conversation.

"Before Thanksgiving. Honestly, I wasn't going to answer his call but curiosity got the better of me."

"Did he apologize at least?"

I nod.

"Is he going to pay you back?" she asks.

I give her a look and she shakes her head.

"But since The Burnt Clovers is doing amazing now, he did ask me to do some more work for them. This time, I was professional about it and drew up a contract and everything."

"Good for you." Indy smacks her fingers against the countertop.

I grin at her, relieved that at least one person in the world would take my side on this. "And he hooked me up with a bunch of other bands who liked my work so…"

"So we don't hate him, but we still strongly dislike him."

"Exactly. I really love the work though, Indy. It's creative and allows me to experiment, to try new things."

Indy smiles at me warmly before reaching across the island to catch my wrist. "That's awesome, Claire. I'm happy for you."

I blush and roll my eyes. "Thanks. But I'm not sure Mom and Dad would see it that way."

"Why not? You're honing your techniques and making some extra money."

"But it's not something I could write into a cover letter. Besides, I could spend that time interning for a lunch stipend. Or networking." I recite Dad's favorite talking points when it comes to my job search.

As much as I enjoy designing logos and collaborating with bands, it's not a career path my family would accept. I bite the corner of my mouth, wondering how much I should divulge to Indy. She's always supported me, but she's also a super smart, disciplined professor with a color-coordinated planner and a detailed five-year plan.

Indy frowns. "You're being too hard on yourself, Claire. Designing logos and collaborating on projects allows you to strengthen your design skills and improve your interpersonal skills. All the things you're doing right now are still steps in the right direction."

I stick my tongue out at Indy. "You're showing your idealistic, professor side. It's very encouraging though. Your students must love you."

Indy tosses her head back and laughs. "One of my students called me Dr. Merrick the other day and I didn't answer. I tell them all to call me Indy."

"You have the perfect job for you."

"You will too. Don't give up on yourself, Claire. You're smart and engaging. You know how to talk to everyone and connect with people effortlessly. You're the full package."

I smile at her gratefully. "Thank you for the pick-me-up chat."

"Thanks for the muffin." She slides from the barstool. "I need to hurry Noah along. We have an ultrasound appointment in an hour."

"Oh my God! Are you going to find out the sex?" I ask, bouncing on my toes.

Indy's eyes gleam. "I am desperate to know."

"You have to call me right after."

She shakes her head. "Noah wants to be surprised."

"Ew," I say, knowing how much my cousin likes to plan and feel prepared for all the things.

"I know," Indy laments. "I have no idea what to buy."

"Neutral colors."

"Boring," she complains.

I roll my eyes and kiss her cheek. "Let me know how you make out at the doctor's."

"Let me know what goes down between you and Broody."

I snort. "Is that what we're calling East now?"

"We need a secret name for him. Everyone knows who he is."

"And Broody is so top-secret, no one would be able to figure it out."

Indy swats at me. "Just tell me when his 'kid' comments become part of foreplay."

"Get out of here." I laugh, walking her toward the staircase where she bellows for Noah.

He appears a moment later, the strap of a duffle bag cutting across his chest. "You ready, babe?"

"All set," Indy says.

"Cool. We'll see you later, Claire. I told East to come over for dinner Friday night. You come too."

"Friday night?"

Noah nods. "Yeah. East's first day back at practice is tomorrow so I figured I'd keep him entertained Friday night since he's used to hitting the bars and clubs with the guys."

"That's a good idea." I shuffle from one foot to the other. "Do you think he'd want me to tag along?"

"Sure. You'll provide an entertaining buffer."

"As long as I'll be useful," I deadpan.

Noah snickers. "At this point, I'll do anything to keep Easton occupied. Too busy to sulk around."

"Your brother is the least cheerful person I know," I agree, pulling open the front door for them.

"He's better with you," Noah says and I can tell he means it. Jeez, for brothers as close as Noah and East are, I can't believe how off-base Noah is about *that*. "See you Friday."

"See you Friday." I wave.

Once they're gone, I walk back into the kitchen. Easton's first day back on the ice is tomorrow. Is he nervous? Excited? Both?

What's it like for the guy who was always the life of the party to avoid it at all costs now? How does Noah plan to keep him distracted? Is he going to invite him over every weekend for dinner?

I frown. Even though Easton and I started our living arrangement on rocky ground, it doesn't mean I don't worry about him. In fact, I still think of him a lot more than I should. Like, all the time. And I do want to help him during this transition.

Pushing my sleeves up on my arms, I dial Mom.

"Claire!" she answers. "I'm so happy you're calling. You and East are coming for dinner on Sunday, right?"

I chuckle. "Yes, Mom. We're in."

"Good. How are you?"

"Good, Mom. I was just wondering, how do you make that chicken piccata recipe?"

"The one Easton likes?" If Mom is surprised, she doesn't show it and my gratitude toward her multiplies.

"That's the one."

"You're cooking dinner?" This time she sounds surprised and I snort.

"Trying, Mom. Just trying. Tomorrow is his first day back on the ice."

"Oh, Claire," Mom's voice softens. "That's very thoughtful of you. Here's what you do…"

I'M NERVOUS. Not my normal, butterfly, jittery, excited nervous but nauseous, I-kind-of-want-to-puke-and-hide nervous. When Easton left for practice this afternoon, he tipped his chin at me in both greeting and farewell.

And my traitorous body reacted all wrong. My mouth watered at the sight of him in worn out sweats and a hoodie. He had a duffle bag strewn over his shoulder and a backwards baseball cap on his head. Two days of scruff coated his cheeks and chin and a haggard kind of tiredness clung to his eyes.

By normal standards, he did not look hot. But by my standards, he looked downright sexy. My fingers tightened into fists, and I held my breath for a word, any word, he threw my way.

I got nada.

The door closed behind him and I spent a solid thirty minutes second-guessing whether I should make him dinner. The plate of muffins is already gone so I know that he doesn't despise my cooking, which is a plus. But I don't want to seem like I'm just hanging around, spending my days doing domestic shit for him. Normal me would kidnap current me for an intervention if that was the case.

He did seem nervous this morning. I know he didn't sleep well last night either because I heard the water running in his shower around three a.m.

Was he fighting his demons? Will he ever confide in me about them? Or does he really hate my being in his space?

I heave a massive sigh and tap my fingers against the countertop.

What do I do? What do I do?

Okay, this is it. I'm going to try one last time to extend an olive branch. I'm going to make Easton dinner, one of his favorite meals, and ask about his practice. I'm going to be thoughtful and considerate and kind.

And if he shuts me down, I'm going to hightail it out of his life so I don't have to endure this daily sinking sensation in my chest of not knowing where I stand with him.

Tonight is the last time I put myself out there for Easton Scotch. So he better accept me now or say goodbye.

Pushing up my sleeves, I get to work on making the best fucking chicken piccata, roasted vegetables, and mashed potatoes number twenty-seven has eaten in his life.

For some reason I'd rather not consider too carefully, my very future seems to depend on it.

CHAPTER 5
EASTON

"You did good today." Austin swats my shoulder as he sits down on the bench beside me in the locker room.

I drag my head up and stare at him.

He winces, his expression sympathetic. "It was your first day back, man. You know this is going to be a long road. You will get back to where you were. But for today, you did good." He smacks the side of my neck before sliding off the bench to see what Torsten is hollering about.

I hang my head, my eyes dropping closed. Shit. I'm sore. My body aches. My head is all kinds of messed up. Dad's face, angry and disappointed, eyes like slits and a mouth that spews venom, flickers to life in my mind.

"You looked good out there," Noah says, sitting down in the spot Austin vacated.

"Cut the bullshit," I grumble, blinking Dad away.

"I'm not bullshitting you. For someone who hasn't done jack shit on the ice for three months, you looked good."

I force my head up at the severity of my brother's tone.

Noah stares me in the eye, willing me to see the truth in his.

I shake my head. "I felt like I was dragging."

"You were."

"Felt slow, sluggish."

Noah nods.

"I'm already sore."

"Ice bath." His lip twitches but he doesn't smile.

"Just say it, man. Whatever you came over here to say." I scrub the back of my neck, trying to loosen the muscles there while I wait for Noah to rip into me.

"I came over to say you looked good out there." Noah drops his voice. "I know you, East. You're beating yourself up over not being the same player you were six months ago. But man, you're not the same guy anymore. You've spent the last ninety days working out in other ways. Dealing with shit, battling our childhood, working through issues. You can't expect to show up and own the rink. You've got to earn that back."

"Yeah," I mutter. I know Noah's right. For the past three months, I've been mentally and emotionally pushing myself, but the physical workouts I'm used to have fallen by the wayside. So has my social life. Of course the guys on the team are happy I'm okay, but that doesn't necessarily mean they're happy I'm back.

I've been too unreliable in the past for them to trust me now. And the guy who took my spot, Sims, well, he's been doing a really bang-up job.

"You, Austin, and I have been playing together a long time." I clear my throat.

Noah nods. The three of us have been *the* offensive line for several seasons.

"But Sims, he's a strong player."

"He is," Noah agrees. "But this isn't about Sims,

Easton. It's about you. If you want your starting position back, if you want to lead the team, if you want what you once had, then you gotta show up and prove it. You hear me?"

I blow out a deep breath, nodding. "Yeah, Noah. I hear you."

"'Kay." Noah slaps my shoulder as he stands up. "I gotta get going. But we're still on for dinner tomorrow night, right?"

"Yeah, I'll be there."

"Good." Noah turns away before stopping and snapping his fingers at me like he just remembered something. "Bring Claire. I already invited her."

"Okay," I say slowly, not understanding why that means we have to be fucking carpool buddies on top of roommates.

"She doesn't have a car," Noah explains, reading my thoughts.

I tip my head back and laugh.

Of course she doesn't. Claire Merrick is everywhere I turn. She's in my thoughts. She's in my house. And last night, I dreamt that she was in my bed.

Why wouldn't she also be coming to Indy and Noah's for dinner?

"Man, she's trying," Noah says softly.

When I look at him, I don't understand the expression on his face. "Whatever, dude. I'll bring her."

Right after I go home and endure another awkward night trying to put distance between us.

I SENSE her the moment I enter the house. It's not just the fact that my winter boots are lined up neatly by the door. Or that the lamp in the living room is turned on. It's none of the little things Noah and I never bothered to do.

It's a feeling. Claire is here and the house feels warmer, safer.

I breathe in and nearly groan at the delicious scents emanating from the kitchen.

Some of the frustration from today's practice lessens now that I'm home, about to have a good meal, and not be alone to get through the night.

"Claire," I call out, dropping my duffel bag to the floor. I pull off my coat and winter hat and take an extra second to hang them where they belong. In fact, I even stow my practice gear.

"In here," she replies. "I made dinner."

"I can tell." I enter the kitchen and my chest constricts at the sight of her, all blonde hair and blue eyes, barefoot, in my kitchen. "It smells amazing."

The tightness around her eyes relaxes and I hate that I've been making her feel like she should walk on eggshells around me. But God, keeping her at a distance is hard.

Maybe I shouldn't try so hard?

I work a swallow and clear my throat.

No, that's insane. I can't let Claire in. If I do, I'll never be able to push her out.

"East?" she asks and I shake my head.

"Sorry?"

"I was just asking how practice went."

I swear and she offers a soft smile. "You've always been too hard on yourself." She turns back to plating our meal.

"What do you mean?" I ask curiously. It's something

I've heard a thousand times before but never from her. Does she pay that much attention to me? To my life? We've hardly spoken in a year.

She lifts two plates and tips her head toward the dining table.

I turn and my breath catches in my throat when I see she's set it all up, a candle burning in the center. Knowing that she spent time doing something nice for me causes my remaining resolve to snap. I know I can't have Claire Merrick, but that doesn't mean I can't know her. Right? I mean, we could be friends. Friendly.

"You didn't have to do all this." I sit where she indicates.

Claire shrugs, placing the dishes down. "I wanted to. Today couldn't have been easy for you."

"It sucked," I agree, glancing up at her. "Chicken piccata's my favorite."

She blushes. "I remember."

I bite my bottom lip. That's twice now. First Claire remembered my hot chocolate and now she made me my favorite meal. Has she always been more tuned into me than I realized? Has she always noticed me as much as I notice her?

She slides into the chair across from mine.

"Thank you, Claire. Really." I dip my chin to make sure she sees the truth in my eyes.

She grins. "It was my pleasure, East."

I stifle a groan just hearing the word *pleasure* roll off her tongue. Jesus, what is wrong with me? This is Austin's baby sister. Joe's daughter.

Claire cuts a piece of chicken and pops it into her mouth. She chews it thoughtfully, her expression careful. "It's not exactly like Mom's."

"No." I shake my head, eating my second bite. "It's better."

Claire beams and I smile back.

"What'd you mean before? About me being too hard on myself?"

"Oh." She flicks her wrist dismissively. "You've always been this way. Don't you remember the skills competition at hockey camp? The one in Muskoka?"

I chuckle, recalling a memory I'd forgotten until Claire jogged it. "The competition between the cabins," I say, remembering that summer in Muskoka, Ontario. It was the summer I met Austin and the rest of the Merricks. "Claire, you were like seven."

"Eight," she corrects me. "But I remember hearing you and Noah and my brother fight over the outcome of that competition for months. You were so angry with yourself for missing that shot."

"It cost us the competition!"

She laughs at my intensity, her eyes twinkling. "Except Austin and Noah missed first."

"Yeah, but it was riding on me. I needed to make the shot."

Claire shakes her head. "It wasn't all on you. It was on them too. You always carry everyone's burdens. What about the time Mom's car ran out of gas in that snowstorm?"

I groan, recalling that night with perfect clarity. The weight of my guilt still sits in the pit of my stomach when I think about it. "I should have filled up her gas tank. I borrowed her car."

Claire shakes her head at me. "East, you borrowed her car *three days* before that snowstorm hit. That wasn't on you."

"It was full when she gave it to me and only three-quarters full when I dropped it off," I say.

Claire smirks. "See what I mean? You find ways to shoulder responsibilities you shouldn't and then you beat yourself up over them. What happened today? On the ice?"

I shake my head, placing my fork down and leaning back in my seat. "I was slow as shit. I missed two goals and got shoved into the boards too many times to count. It felt like Austin and Noah were covering for me."

"Oh, so you played like someone who hasn't played in three months?"

I smirk at the sarcasm in her voice. "Listen smartass, my entire future is resting on this moment. This season. If I don't perform, the Hawks might not resign me next year."

"You're contract is up?" she asks, her mouth dropping open as it clicks.

"In ten months."

"Then you've got ten months to sort out your shit, Scotch. But no way in hell are you playing anywhere but Boston."

I laugh at the resolve in her tone. "Just like that, huh Claire?"

"Just like that. You can throw your little pity party for the rest of the night, but tomorrow, you get back on the ice and start working toward what you want."

I run my hand over my jaw, grinning at her. She's so beautiful in the candlelight. Her eyes sparkle, her mouth purses thoughtfully but it's her presence that shifts the energy of the house. Just having her here infuses my veins with a bit of optimism when I've been filling them with poison for too long.

She catches me looking at her and smiles softly, shyly. It's so damn sweet I want to remember it for always. Claire has always had a larger-than-life personality. She's a force in any social setting. But sometimes, when it's just the two of us, she relaxes a little, some of her hype releases, and she's too tender for her own good.

"I'm glad you're here, Claire." I mean it too.

One side of her mouth pulls up. "Me too. Life with Mama and Daddy Merrick is stricter than rehab."

I snort, shaking my head at her. Everyone I know avoids talking about rehab like it's a trigger for me. Everyone except Claire who cracks a joke about it. "You think so, do you?"

"How was it, really?"

"You're the first person to ask me that."

"So tell me."

I chew the corner of my mouth, considering my words. If anyone else asked, I'd toss out some generic bullshit about it being tough but necessary, an important learning experience on my recovery journey. But at the compassion, not pity, in Claire's eyes, I admit the truth. "It fucking sucked. It was hard. Every damn day felt like a battle I'd most likely lose. It still feels that way. Like I'm constantly fighting to push water uphill. To not screw everything up."

Claire leans forward, her expression serious. "I'm proud of you, Easton."

I snicker, covering up the slice that rips through my chest at her words. "For what? I haven't done anything worth being proud of, Claire."

"That's not true." She shakes her head and bites her bottom lip. "If that were true, then neither have I."

"What?" I sit up straight. "This again? What are you talking about?"

"Look at me, East."

"I am." I let my gaze scan her face.

"That's not what I meant." She grins before sobering again. "I'm a twenty-four-year-old, unemployed mess. Up until last week and the generosity of you and Noah, I still lived at home with my parents. They pay for my phone bill. I'm painfully single. Every time I go out and meet a guy, we click no problem. We go on a handful of dates but nothing ever comes of it. My best friend Rielle is a workaholic, my sister moved to New York, and Indy is pregnant." She shrugs, her eyes flaring with an emotion I can't place.

I hold my breath, a lump forming in my throat.

"I feel like everyone in my life is five steps ahead of me and no matter how hard I try, I can't catch up. So if you feel like I shouldn't be proud of you, someone who's made it in his career of choice, someone who has financial stability without anyone else's help, someone who's owned up to his mistakes and taken active steps to rectify them, someone who tries every single day to do the right thing, then where does that leave me?"

CHAPTER 6
CLAIRE

Easton's mouth twists at my words, anger rippling over his expression. "Don't try to make me feel better, Claire."

"I'm not." Okay, maybe I am…but just a little.

Easton shakes his head. "You're more than I'll ever be. I know you're bummed right now about not having the perfect job. And yeah, I get how much it sucks that everyone in your circle seems to be moving forward and you feel stuck. But Claire, trust me"—he looks directly into my eyes, a gravity to his stare I've never felt before—"it just means something bigger and better is coming for you."

I snort and raise an eyebrow. "Now who's trying to make who feel better?"

Easton's eyes glimmer as he leans back in his chair. He runs his hand over his forehead, his finger catching on the scar that splits his eyebrow. He always rubs it when he's nervous, unsure, or downright angry. What is he right now? "I promise you, Claire, we are nothing alike."

His words are honest but they still scrape at my soul. I

know we're nothing alike. Easton is a guy who could have the world at his fingertips if he so desires. And I'm me, the kid that everyone worries about and indulges. "Yeah, I know."

At my tone, his eyes darken, Mediterranean blue. "I didn't mean…" He shakes his head. "That's twice now that you've misunderstood my words. I'm not explaining myself well." He sighs. "You're a better person than I'll ever be, Claire. That's what I mean when I say we aren't alike. And I'm happy you're here. Really. I'm sorry I didn't make you feel welcome the way I should've."

At his confession my eyes pop and my mouth falls open. Some of the hurt I was preparing to wallow in dissipates. "Seriously?"

He scowls at me. "What do you mean? Of course I'm being serious."

"Well you sure did a killer job rolling out the welcoming committee."

Easton laughs. "I'm sorry I was a dick to you."

"Wow, what is happening? An apology? From Easton Scotch." Embarrassment blooms in his face and I laugh, pointing at him. "Now, you're blushing."

"I forgot what a pain in the ass you are."

I smirk, my heart thumping at his reaction. "You really don't hate having me around?"

He scrapes a hand along his jawline. "Not as much as I should."

Uh, what? I narrow my gaze, asking what the hell that means, but Easton spears another piece of chicken and sets it on his plate. "Tell me about all these jobs you're applying for."

"Wait, what?" I try to catch up to what just happened and how he thought that subject change was subtle. It was jarring.

Easton chews a piece of chicken. "These jobs. Why are you applying for so many? I find it hard to believe you're not qualified for anything."

I flip him the middle finger and he snickers. "I'd say it was a tough job market but I feel like that's everyone's excuse," I mutter.

He looks up, his gaze sharpening. "It *is* a tough job market."

"Whatever," I sigh, grabbing another piece of chicken.

Easton regards me thoughtfully. "If you could do any job you want, have any position, what would it be?"

"Why?" I ask slowly.

"Holy shit, you're distrustful. I don't remember you being this skeptical, Claire."

"I don't remember you being so dismissive and aloof either," I shoot back.

He sighs. His gaze lingers on mine as he chews the corner of his mouth. "You're right. I have been a dick to you, to most people, since the first time I went to rehab. I guess a lot has changed in the past year."

"Why?" I ask, genuinely curious.

"Because I messed everything up, Claire." His voice is gruff. He clenches the fork before it clatters to the plate. "I am a fuckup. And you, you would always look at me like I'm this great guy—"

"You are a great guy."

"Like I somehow didn't disappoint every single member of your family."

"You didn't disappoint me."

He snaps his mouth closed and lifts his eyebrows.

I wince at the dare in his eyes. "Fine, you did disappoint me when you stopped talking to me. We used to be friends, East. You used to look out for me."

"I'm looking out for you right now," he shoots back

and I can tell I hit a nerve because his mouth tightens and his eyes blaze. "I'm protecting you from me."

From him? Is he delusional? Other than my feelings, I know Easton would never intentionally hurt me. "What if I don't want you to?" I whisper, my voice huskier than I intend. My thighs clench together as I stare at Easton. Intensity rolls off of him in waves and I wish, not for the first time, that I could drown in it. In him.

He swears and shakes his head, breaking the momentary spell. "I'm sorry I was shitty."

I shrug.

"I mean it. You didn't have to do this." He points to the dinner I made.

"I wanted to do something nice for you," I admit.

"I know, Claire." His expression softens. "You always do right by me, kid. I really hate that I hurt your feelings. I never meant to."

The "kid" bit stings but the rest of it, the sincerity in his tone and the truth in his eyes, acts as a salve. "Apology accepted," I mumble.

Easton catches my eyes. "Tell me about your dream job."

"Okay," I agree. "I would own my own business."

He rears back, his surprise evident.

I snort. "Weren't expecting that, were you?"

He shakes his head and at least it's honest.

I wrinkle my nose. "Everyone always underestimates me."

Easton freezes, his nostrils flaring as if I've pissed him off. "I didn't mean it like that, Claire."

I lift a hand to stop him but he shakes his head.

"No, really," he says. "I think you can do anything you want. Absolutely anything. I've just never heard you mention your own business before. You always talked about design. Then you went through that animation obsession, remember?" He chuckles. "You only wanted to work for Disney. So much so that you were going to apply to be a character at the Magic Kingdom and 'work your way up.'"

I laugh, recalling a whole summer where I practiced being Aurora and Cinderella, all of the blonde Disney princesses. "I can't believe you remember that."

He nods, his eyes shining. "I remember, Claire. After that you were going to design wallpaper."

"Oh my God!" I facepalm. "That was because of that one class I took."

Easton nods, knowingly. "Introduction to Modern Design."

"Yes!" I point at him in disbelief. "I forgot all about that crazy professor."

"Dr. P," we say at the same time.

Easton grins and I smile back. My chest warms from the memories and also from Easton recalling them, as if he cared all along.

"You never said anything about your own business," he reminds me.

I sigh. "I guess I never did. It's a newer idea since I've started designing band logos. It started more as a hobby. Mainly because of my fangirling but—"

"Hold up." East lifts his hand. "Who are you fangirling over?"

My blush deepens. "I dated a musician over the summer."

His eyebrows furrow for a moment but then realization sweeps over his expression and his eyes harden. "Derek."

"Derek," I agree.

Easton watches me for a second, his gaze intense. I shift

under his scrutiny, desperate for him to say something. "Are you still a *fan*?"

I snort out a laugh, breaking some of the tension between us. "Absolutely not. But Derek's introduced me to other bands and several of them have reached out over the past two months."

He chews his chicken thoughtfully. "Any bands I'd know?"

I stall by taking a large gulp of water. There's no way Easton hasn't heard of Derek Reiner because The Burnt Clovers is the biggest indie band to come out of Boston in the last five years. Talking about dating or guys is uncharted territory for Easton and me and I suddenly feel nervous.

Across the table, he lifts his eyebrows, waiting.

"Well, Derek is the lead singer for The Burnt Clovers."

Recognition flares in his eyes. "You *dated* Derek Reiner?"

I wave a hand again, trying for dismissive. "It was casual."

"How casual?" he asks way too quickly.

I roll my eyes. "I'm still doing some work for them. But I'm also doing a new logo for Sanders Street—"

"The rock group?"

I nod. "And Kellman's Kiss."

Easton whistles, looking impressed.

"I met a few other guys at an open mic night," I blurt out. "Come spring, I need to start hitting up the music festivals."

"So, this is something you want to do for real?" Easton's eyebrows snap together.

I bite my bottom lip. What am I even saying? Hopefully, by spring, I'll be gainfully employed. Right? Isn't that the goal? I shrug. "I guess, if I could, I would turn this into a full-time thing and start my own business."

"Claire, those bands are heavy-hitters. Especially The Burnt Clovers. If you've managed all this in just a few months, why don't you try? See where it goes?"

I take a sip of my water and clear my throat. "Um, have you met my dad?"

"Joe's holding you back?"

"He just paid for me to go to college."

"So? You're using your degree. You're applying it to something you love doing."

"I don't know…Dad is pretty insistent that I find a real job where I have a 401k and benefits."

Easton tilts his head to the side. "There are more things to life than a retirement plan and benefits."

"Says the person with a fat savings account and the best medical coverage."

He snickers. "Fair enough. How 'bout this? You keep doing your designs while applying to jobs. And I'll keep grinding on the ice even though it feels like a losing battle. And we'll prop each other up when one of us gets too low." He raises his eyebrow with the scar and I hang onto the flicker of vulnerability in his blue eyes.

"Deal," I say softly.

"Deal," he repeats.

I point the tines of my fork at him. "So, just to be clear, you want to be real friends again?"

He chuckles, shaking his head. "You really are a pain in the ass, Claire."

"Yeah, but I've got a great ass so…" I joke.

Easton laughs again but it's strained this time. His eyes are both amused and serious when they meet mine. "Stand up and turn around," he dares. "I'll let you know."

I flip him the middle finger again and this time, we

both laugh. The space between us hums with a familiarity I crave. Nostalgia washes over me and I beam at Easton, relieved that we've reconnected again. The tense, awkward exchanges I've danced around for the past year give way to a comfortable rapport that I've missed.

I eat another bite of chicken piccata, relieved that I decided to put myself out there one last time. Because for the first time in over a year, it seems like I've found my footing with Easton again. Tonight feels like old times. He's the man I remember, funny and engaging.

His grin is easy and his eyes are warm as they watch me from across the dining table. My heartbeat ticks up and I squirm as a rush of heat shoots through me. I'm not going to lie; I could get used to this.

But I always knew that Easton Scotch was it for me. Even if he has no clue.

CHAPTER 7

EASTON

I never thought I'd be nervous to go to dinner at my brother's. But I am. It seems less like a casual dinner, back when Noah and I would shoot the shit with a beer in hand, and more like a test.

Noah and Indy are the real deal. They have something my brother never had with his ex-fiancée Courtney and it was evident the second I saw them together. He looks at Indy like she's his forever and she hangs onto every word he says like it's going to solve climate change.

I've known Indy for years but other than a handful of conversations, I've never really kicked it with her. Now, I want her to like me. I want her to want me as part of the family she's growing with my brother.

"You clean up nice." Claire bounds down the steps, meeting me in the foyer.

My mouth dries as I get a good look at her. Damn, she's gorgeous. She looks like she's gearing up to walk down a runway instead of heading to her cousin's house for dinner. She's dressed in skintight black leather leggings that leave nothing to the imagination and an off-the-shoulder sweater. Her ass is round and pert, the leather stretching as she bends to retrieve her boots. I swallow back my groan, my hands desperate to palm the sweet globes of her ass. Her sweater slips down her shoulder as she turns, offering her smooth skin up like a present I can never have. She straightened her hair, golden strands that fall to the center of her back, and her makeup makes her eyes pop.

Shit. I shift my weight, trying to readjust myself as I harden just checking her out. What the hell is wrong with me? This is Claire Merrick, Austin's kid sister. My new friend.

I can't think of her this way. And yet, when she stands with her heeled boots strapped to her feet, adding nearly three inches to her height, I want nothing more than to pull her against my chest and drag my mouth over hers.

Oblivious to my thoughts, she pulls on her winter coat, tying the sash around her waist. Then she picks up a box of pastries. "You all ready?"

I clear my throat, hot and uncomfortable. "Yeah. Let's go."

I keep a close eye on Claire as we walk down the icy path to my car. It wouldn't take much for her to fall flat on her back in those boots. "Careful in those shoes."

She smirks at me over her shoulder, rolling her eyes. "Showing your age, Scotch."

"What? I'm only twenty-nine."

"Almost the big three-oh," she reminds me just as she wobbles, throwing her arm out to find balance.

I grip her arm before she falls and pull her body against mine. My arm wraps around her waist, my hand settling on her hip. She looks up at me, her eyes wide, a flare of nerves from her near fall. "You almost wiped out there, Clairebear."

Her lips curl at the old nickname I haven't used in years. Maybe even a decade. "*Almost* being the operative word there."

"You would have bit it if I wasn't here. Messed up this hot look you're rocking."

Her mouth purses, wisps of smoke appearing in the cold. "You think I'm hot, Easton?"

Shit. I'm playing with fire and I know it. But instead of letting the flames turn to embers, I'm fanning them to swell into an inferno. "You don't need compliments from me, Claire. You know you're beautiful."

She drops her gaze, her eyes staring at the hollow of my throat. Can she tell that just being this close to her makes my heart pump faster? I should drop my arm. I don't.

Claire steps out of my hold and offers a small smile. "Still nice to hear it every now and then."

I smile back. "You look beautiful tonight, Claire."

"Thank you." She opens the car door and slips into the passenger seat.

Jesus, Scotch, pull your shit together. You've barely been out of rehab two weeks and you're already blurring lines.

I climb into my car, flip the ignition, and pull out toward my brother and Indy's place.

"Did you miss driving? When you were in rehab?" Claire asks me.

Palming the steering wheel, I glance at her. "Yeah. Honestly, I'm just glad they didn't take my license away. Of all the fuckups I made, a DUI was never one of them."

"Well, that's a relief," she quips sarcastically.

"Why don't you have a car?"

She lifts an eyebrow. "Seriously? My parents are still paying my cell phone bill."

I shake my head. "What about the money you saved? The money you offered to pay rent with."

She's quiet for a long moment. "I was kind of banking on you and Noah not asking me for rent money."

I laugh, glancing at her from the corner of my eye. "You know we would never." I pause, a new thought coming to mind. "Do you even have a savings account?"

"I do but I'm new to the saving game," she admits quietly.

I bite back the urge to laugh. "Meaning?"

"I'm a fuckup too, East. I blew it all on booze and nights out."

My head whips toward her. "Seriously?"

She wiggles her eyebrows but her eyes have a haunted look that pisses me off. "Yeah. It was stupid." She turns to glance out the window. "Summer was…summer. Reality came crashing down in September."

From her dismissal, I feel like there's more to the story. For an entire city block, we're quiet, lost in our thoughts. But the more seconds that tick by, the more my curiosity eats at me like a bulldog until I blurt out, "Who was the guy?" Please don't say Reiner.

"Hm?"

"Who was the guy you were trying to impress?" I bite out, pissed off that she blew through her savings account to get some douchebag's attention. Even more pissed off because I already know who he is. A musician with rock star appeal.

She rolls her eyes. "What if I just went out to enjoy myself and have a bunch of girls' nights?"

"I don't buy it. That's not the full story."

She huffs, "Fine. It was Derek and it was stupid." She shrugs but I see the way her shoulders dip closer, as if she's protecting herself. Is that because of something he did? Or her embarrassment over the situation?

"What happened, Claire?" I bite out, clenching the steering wheel tighter.

She huffs out a deep breath. "There were a few instances but the one that really sticks out is when he stuck me with a dinner bill for about nine people."

I work a swallow and turn to glare at her.

"At Carters," she whispers.

"Shit." I shake my head. I didn't like Derek the second she mentioned him. Now, I can't stand the guy. Anger rushes through me at the thought of her getting played by a freaking *singer*. And then again at the realization that they still talk, that she's *working* for him. "Sounds like a real winner, Claire." My tone is hard. I grip the steering wheel tighter, my knuckles popping.

"I said it was stupid," she whispers.

"Austin know?" I ask, barely containing my anger.

She whips her head around. "No. And don't tell him. He'll be so pissed at me. Same with my parents. I had to tell them that I spent the money on an extra course."

I pinch the bridge of my nose, turning over these details. On the one hand, I'm glad she's confiding in me. Giving me the truth when she clearly glossed over the details with her family. She's allowing herself to be real with me, even if she's embarrassed, and I like that she trusts me. On the other hand, I want to throttle Derek for taking advantage of her kindness and scold her for falling for his play.

I blow out a breath. "Derek contacts you again, outside of a professional capacity, you tell me."

"What? Why?"

"Because."

In my peripheral vision, I see that she widens her eyes at me but I don't turn to meet them.

"Anyway," she sighs, "that's why I don't have a car. Trust me, after graduation and one sick summer, I've been slapped in the face with a brutal reality check."

I sigh, letting my temper cool. I hear the undercurrent of dejection in Claire's tone and relate to it. To her. "I hear you, kid. It's been the same for me since getting out of rehab the first time. The past year has been tough."

Claire is quiet for a moment and I can taste the intensity of her curiosity. "What's it like, East?"

"What's what like?"

"Having an addiction? Do you feel it all the time?"

My throat burns at her words and I nod once. "It's like choking on sand. In the beginning, it fills your throat so quickly that you're panicked, nearly out of your mind with need for oxygen, for alcohol. With each passing day, it gets a little easier, a little less intense. You learn to breathe around it, to cope, to distract yourself." I shrug, peering over at her. "But there are always triggers."

She's solemn as she stares at me. "What are your triggers?"

I blow out a laugh, shaking my head, as I pull in front of my brother's new place, Indy's tenement apartment building. Dad's voice blares in my head and I shake him away. "That's a story for another day, Clairebear. We're here." I park and turn off the car.

For several moments, we sit in silence, looking at each other. In the past two days, Claire and I have shared a lot. Truths, embarrassments, denials. We've spoken them aloud, knowing the other person would pluck them from the air and tuck them away for safekeeping.

It's strange because for an entire year, I barely saw Claire.

Now, in the matter of two weeks, I can't imagine this period of my life without her. She's a lightness, a breath of fresh air, a flicker of hope, in a void of darkness. A look of understanding passes between us, and Claire smiles at me, sweet and sincere.

I tip my head toward the apartment. "You ready?"

She nods, picking up the box of pastries she bought for dessert. It's sweet, considering she barely has two nickels to rub together. But that's the thing with Claire; even though she pretends otherwise, she's always putting everyone before herself.

"Let's go, Scotch." She climbs from the car.

I hold back a minute so I can enjoy the view of her ass all the way to Indy and Noah's apartment door.

CHAPTER 8
CLAIRE

"You and Broody seem to be getting along great." Indy wags her eyebrows at me. "He even seems less broody."

"I hate to tell you this but I don't think Broody as a nickname is going to stick."

Indy snorts. "Tell me everything." My cousin pinches my side as I step around her and duck behind the refrigerator door, searching for the sparkling water Indy bought.

"It's fine," I whisper.

"How fine?" Her eyes glitter.

"Fine, fine."

"How was the dinner you made him?"

I narrow my eyes and stand from my crouched position, sparkling water in hand. "How do you know about that?"

"Your mom called me."

"Of course she did."

"And Noah told me."

"Noah?" I ask, surprised. Does that mean Easton told his brother that I—

"Easton called him last night and they talked. That was really nice of you, Claire. Noah said it meant a lot to East." At her words, warmth rolls through my chest. Sure, Easton and I are getting along now—we're friends—but it's still nice to know that my olive branch meant something.

"Good. That's good."

"I'd say that's great. Besides, he hasn't stopped looking over here since you came into the kitchen. Don't look." Indy throws out a hand to stop me from turning.

"He probably thinks we're talking about him."

She shrugs. "We *are* talking about him."

Indy and I both start laughing.

"See, I really am a genius." She pokes at me and I roll my eyes.

"Fine, I'm going to give you this one. It was a good idea, Indiana."

"Please, it was better than good." My cousin takes the sparkling water from my hand. "Now go sit down. Dinner is served."

I slide into a chair at the kitchen table as Easton sits beside me. Noah helps Indy bring dinner to the table and I watch as Easton tracks every movement, his expression thoughtful.

Once we're all seated, Indy springs into action by fixing our plates, piling them with turkey, mashed potatoes, and cauliflower and carrots. Something I don't understand crosses Easton's expression, similar to the look he gave me yesterday at dinner. It's a mix between gratitude and longing.

Are his homemade meals so few and far between? He must feel me looking at him because he glances my way, his expression smoothing out when our eyes meet.

"So, Easton," Indy says and East stiffens beside me. "Did Noah tell you how he almost botched our relationship before it got off the ground?" She lifts an eyebrow and I feel the tension drain from Easton's body as he chuckles.

"Indy girl, I knew my brother was feeling you from the first night he saw you at Firefly. I called him the next morning and he couldn't believe he had his head so far up his ass that he missed the part where you'd moved to Boston."

Indy laughs and looks at Noah.

Noah lifts his chin at his brother. "Way to throw me under the bus."

East shrugs, a grin playing over his mouth. "I gotta get in tight with Indy. She's the one who will be controlling Little Scotch's social calendar."

Noah laughs and Indy beams.

East asks, "How are you feeling, anyway?"

As Indy launches into a very detailed explanation of the myriad of pregnancy symptoms she's experiencing—truly, her story could serve as a form of birth control to the next generation—Easton drops some of his hardness. The longer he chats with Noah, the more he seems to relax. Each time Indy's laughter rings out, he smiles. Little by little, he melts back into the boy I remember from my teenage years, the one I saw a glimpse of last night. A surge of bittersweet nostalgia fills my veins. *That* guy still exists.

"How's the job hunt, Claire?" Noah asks me, shifting the conversation.

I wince, flipping him the thumbs-up.

"That good, huh?" he jokes.

I shrug, taking a sip of my sparkling water. "The rejection letters are piling up. I may start scrapbooking them."

Noah shoots me a sympathetic look as Indy wrinkles her nose.

Easton shifts next to me and wraps his arm around the back of my chair, his hand hanging over the top. I freeze. His fingers are only inches from my neck and the proximity of his touch has my body spiraling into overdrive. His fingernails skate across my hair, featherlight and so fleeting, I don't know if it happened or I wished it into existence.

God, what is wrong with me? Easton and I are good. We're friends again. Why can't that be enough?

"Claire's got too many great ideas to be saddled with a nine-to-five anyway," Easton declares and my stomach drops to my toes.

"What do you mean?" Indy asks curiously.

"She's designing all these awesome band logos and merchandise. I don't know why she doesn't do her own thing instead of searching for some position that will squash her creativity."

"Is your demand picking up?" Excitement fills Indy's expression.

I feel Easton's gaze on the side of my face as I try to quell the nerves buzzing through my body. I know he didn't mean to out me in front of my cousin and Noah. It's not like Indy didn't know about my new passion project.

It's just that, I never let Indy think my current paying gigs were something I'd consider making a career out of. There's no way my parents would support me trying to go out on my own. There's no way my cousin who I adore like a sister would understand when her whole life has been dictated by measurement units like grades and rankings. She thrives on knowing her role in a larger system.

Besides, who am I to just create the role I want? I'm twenty-four years old with my parents paying my cell phone bill and Noah and Easton allowing me to live rent-free.

Easton's arm locks down behind my head. His glance on my face turns into a glare as he waits for me to say something. I feel the shift in his energy and I hate that I'm somehow causing him stress.

Forcing a smile, I clear my throat and nod. "Yeah. I've had three new bands reach out in the past two days. With so many unfulfilled hours, it keeps me busy. I'm working on my photoshop skills and learning new lighting techniques."

Indy nods, her mouth pursed as if she's thinking this over. Noah leans back in his chair and asks, "Why don't you run with that, Claire? I mean, if you like it, why not make that your main focus?"

Easton relaxes slightly.

Indy frowns, shaking her head. "Uncle Joe would lose it."

My heart sinks a little at the truth in her words, a fresh reminder just how much my family would rebuke any attempt I make to carve my own path. It's not that they wouldn't support my desire to create and experiment and try. It's that they wouldn't want that to fill the role of my "real job." Because a real job is supposed to provide security, benefits, and a 401k.

"Why?" Noah asks, shaking his head. "Your uncle is a rational man. If Claire loves working with bands, being in the music industry, why shouldn't she give that a go?"

Easton leans closer to the table, as if drawn to the answer.

I hold my breath, hating this conversation more with each passing second. I'm usually great in social settings. I know how to draw the fun and flirty attention my way and deflect the questions that delve deeper into my goals, plans, or dreams. I hate putting myself out there and having people know things about me that make me feel vulnerable. That's why I only told Indy about creating logos. And then Easton because I was trying to cheer him up after his hockey practice.

Indy shakes her head, wrinkling her nose at me before turning to Noah. "I'll support anything Claire wants, but Uncle Joe and Aunt Mary will be a hard sell. Owning a small business is a lot of work. There are so many variables, so much instability. I'm not saying Uncle Joe wouldn't be behind Claire doing something she loves. Just that he would want to see her more settled, with a job that offers more guarantees." Indy glances at me again. "Don't you think?"

She speaks the truth. I hate that she knows my parents' response as well as I do. I paste on a smile. "Yeah, he's all about that retirement plan."

Noah chuckles and Indy shoots me a sympathetic look. The conversation turns to my sister Savannah's teaching position in New York. I look down at my plate, my appetite having vanished over the last ten minutes. Suddenly, my stomach is in knots and a sense of dread washes through my limbs.

For so many months, I've been focused on securing a job that I never really cared if it was *the* job. What if I spend my whole life doing something I don't love just because it checks all the boxes?

But whose boxes?

I startle at Easton's touch. His fingers slide through my hair so unexpectedly that my body short-circuits. I look over at him but his eyes are trained on Indy as she continues on about Savannah, her husband Mike, and their lives in New York.

Easton's fingertips brush against the back of my neck slowly. I glance at Noah but he's watching my cousin, so completely enamored by her that I don't know if he'd notice an asteroid crashing into the center of the dining table.

Easton's fingers make one pass, then again, then they wrap around the back of my neck and squeeze gently.

Noah laughs at something Indy says. She smiles at him sweetly. Easton leans into my side and drops his voice so only I can hear. "Don't give up on your daydreams, Clairebear."

I shiver as his breath rolls over the side of my face. Of course he would detect that Indy's words affected me. But how? My family, sometimes even my best friend Rielle, all seem oblivious to how much my heart isn't into the traditional job hunt.

How does Easton understand in a handful of weeks?

His hand slips away and immediately, a chill replaces the warmth of his touch.

I force a bite of turkey, chewing slowly as I mull over Easton's words. Does he think applying for other jobs is giving up on myself? Everyone's thoughts about *my* future seem surer than my own. Their certainty in the right path causes my footing to slip, as if I don't know the right way forward.

Dinner continues without a hitch. Noah and East have us all cracking up with stories of previous hockey seasons, of silly pranks gone wrong. Indy shares how all the Hawks players are enamored with me. Noah confirms this and I duck my head, blushing a furious shade of red, as East glances at me, his expression amused, his eyes thoughtful.

Too soon, we're saying good night. As East and I walk to his car, his hand wraps around my arm protectively and hope flares in my ribs, rushing up to my chest. I feel tipsy from his touch. Intoxicated by how in sync Easton and I are. He *sees* me, he understands the fragility of my feelings when it comes to my future, and he supports me.

For years, it felt like everyone overlooked me. Saw past me. Savannah was the socializing beauty. Austin the hockey god. Indy the smarty-pants brainiac.

I was always just the silly kid. But tonight, Easton saw more than that. And he defended it.

"You have a good time?" he asks, pulling away from the curb.

"Yeah. Tonight was fun. You?"

East nods, tapping his palm against the steering wheel. "It's been a good couple of days."

"For me too," I agree, happy we're in a good place.

When we get home, East locks the door behind us. He stares at me for a long moment as I hang up my coat and place my boots in the hall closet. I raise my eyebrows at him, waiting for him to say whatever he's thinking.

But he shakes his head, an enigmatic expression crossing his features. "Night, Clairebear."

"Good night, East."

AFTER THAT NIGHT, an easiness settles between Easton and me. We morph from two strangers with a shared connection to two friends living together. During the day, East sticks to a rigorous schedule of workouts, practices, AA meetings, and group therapy. I apply for jobs every morning, casting a wide net for positions spanning across the country. But in the afternoons, after lunch, I feed my creative side by designing album cover concepts and logo templates and posting them in an online group I created. Some nights, I cook dinner. Most nights, we scrap something together or order out. At night, we play cards or Netflix and chill. Really chill, not code word *chill*.

For two weeks, our routine is natural and fun. We talk, we laugh, we hang out. But we don't cross any lines. Although I'd be lying if I said we didn't begin to blur and smudge them. But how could I not with Easton living right down the hall?

Every morning, the sight of his bare chest and bedhead make my mouth water. The colorful ink that scrolls up the left side of his body has my fingers tingling with the need to touch. Once, he walked out of his bedroom with just a towel wrapped around his waist and I literally drooled. "Eyes up here, Clairebear," he taunted. So yeah, I'm not saying living with Easton and keeping things strictly platonic is easy or anything.

But we're doing it. Until we're not.

CHAPTER 9
EASTON

I open the door to my locker. The noose that's been tightening around my neck all week loosens a hair. Today felt okay. For the first time since I left rehab, I was back on the ice and didn't feel sluggish, off-balanced, or terrified.

"Nice work today, East." Torsten slaps me on the back.

"Thanks, man."

"You looked good," he adds. I know he means it too. Torsten is the oldest guy on the team, and over the past few years, his outlook has shifted. He's morphed from protecting his playing time with the ferocity of a Viking to mentoring the younger guys as we come up the ranks.

"You too."

He snorts.

"What?" I ask, rubbing a towel over my wet hair.

"It's a relief to hear you say it, East. Because I am feeling the hits from the other night's game. My body does not recover the way it used to."

I frown, recalling the two solid hits Torsten took in

Tuesday night's game. He started but wasn't able to finish the third period.

"You all right?" I ask, lowering my voice. Injury can be the kiss of death.

Torsten nods, chuckling. "More than all right, East. You're back, the team's jiving, and I played hard this week."

Some of my worry eases at his words and I grin. "Good. What're you getting into now?"

Torsten shrugs, pulling open a locker door a few down from mine and starting to dress. "Gonna eat something. You hungry?"

I pull a sweater over my head. "Could always eat, Big Daddy."

He snorts. "Want to grab a bite?"

"Sure," I answer automatically. Before, I used to grab bites and happy hours with the guys all the time. But this is the first time any of the guys on the team, not counting my brother or Austin, have asked me to hang out since rehab.

I recognize the olive branch for what it is and I jump on it, not wanting to miss an opportunity to remind the guys that I'm committed to the team, to this season, to them.

"Cool. Panda's in too," Torsten says, mentioning our goalie.

"Ryan?" I ask about the other starting defenseman.

Torsten shakes his head, giving me a sad smile. It's no secret that James Ryan has been struggling for the last year. His wife's death rocked him to his core and raising twins on his own has taken its toll. Other than his commitment to the team, he rarely socializes. He shows up, puts in the work, and rushes home to his kids.

"How's he doing?" I ask.

Torsten sighs, his expression somber. "Good days and bad. It hasn't been an easy year."

I pull a sweater over my head. No, it certainly has not.

Once we're dressed, we leave the arena and head to the parking lot.

"Follow me." Torsten points down the road. "There's a little place I like in the West End." He glances at me over his shoulder. "It's not too far from your brother and Indy. See if Noah wants to come."

I shake my head. "He's busy today." Not wanting to share my brother's personal life, I don't add that he's accompanying Indy to the doctor's for an ultrasound.

Torsten shrugs. "Okay."

I get behind the wheel of my car and follow Torsten and Panda through the busy city streets until we pull up to the eclectic, bright, Mexican fusion restaurant. Even though I've only been here once, my mouth waters the moment I recognize the place. The food is *that* good.

The guys and I make our way into the restaurant and Torsten leads us to a table in the back. A few patrons glance at us as we weave through the tables. Several hushed whispers break out and I feel the hair on the back of my neck stand at attention. Are they whispering about Hawks players being here? Or are they dissecting all my screwups, wondering aloud how many more months until I'm back in rehab?

The thought rattles me even though it surfaces in my mind several times a day. Some days, multiple times an hour. My throat burns and my heart pounds in my temples as I feel the eyes of strangers tracking my movements.

I'm relieved when I'm seated at the table, my back to the restaurant and all of the attention I don't want.

Panda sighs as he unfolds his large body into a chair. "Man, this week has been brutal."

Torsten snickers. "I was just telling East in the locker room that my body doesn't recover the way it used to."

Panda shoots me an amused grin. "East is still too young to know what that's like."

I flip him the middle finger and he chuckles. Relief rolls through my veins at their ribbing. For years, Torsten and Panda gave me shit for being green and wet behind the ears. The fact that they're doing it now, after all the stress and shit I caused the team, feels good. Normal.

The same server as last time pops by. "Hey guys! I'm Shell and I'll be your server today."

"Hey Shell." Torsten smiles at her like they've been friends for years and Panda rolls his eyes.

"Hi, Torsten. Good game on Tuesday." Shell grins back and Panda and I both hide our laughter.

Torsten shakes his head at us. "You could both be a little friendlier," he scolds us in front of Shell.

Shell chuckles. "Can I get you guys something to drink?"

Immediately, a tension forms, hovering over the table like a storm cloud. Torsten and Panda glance at me, their gazes flickering with an uncertainty that causes the burn in my throat to increase tenfold. My shoulders stiffen. Shit.

"You guys order whatever you want," I say, waving a hand. I keep my tone light, my gestures easygoing. But inside, the monster within roars to life. My eyes dart to the bar, to the taps of beer, to the bottles on bottles of alcohol. My chest tightens, my throat now on fire. I shift my hands to my knees, clenching the fabric of my jeans. "I'll take an iced tea."

Panda's eyes narrow. "You sure, East?"

I nod, smiling at him. At least, I try to smile. "Of course, man."

Whatever he sees in my expression puts him at ease.

It's both a testament to what a skilled bullshitter I am as much as it is to how no one truly understands the demons I'm constantly warring with.

Today feels different than the lunch after I left rehab. I'm not with family now, but with teammates. Sure, they're like family, but the dynamic is different. These are the guys I used to get shitfaced with. The guys who would carry my drunk ass home. Anxiety claws up my throat and my heart hammers.

"Sweet." Panda's gaze shifts to Shell. "I'll take a Corona."

"Make it two." Torsten throws up two fingers.

Shell runs through a couple of specials I don't hear because a roaring sound, like an ocean wave, fills my ears. The eyes on my back intensify until it feels like an entire arena of people are watching my every move, waiting for me to slip up, to fuck up. *Again.*

Dad's voice, his cold blue eyes so much like mine, flicker in and out of my head.

Panda and Torsten study the menu. My eyes are locked on Shell, on the tray with the two cold, tangy beers resting on top. The limes stick out the tops of the bottles and my mouth waters, imagining the taste of the cold beer with a hint of lime.

My teeth clamp down, my molars grinding together. I force my gaze to the menu, scanning it for something to distract me, but nothing can distract me from the clink of ice in an empty glass, the colorful bottles on shelves behind the bar, the loud laughter of a toast a few tables over.

"Here you go." Shell returns and sound rushes back.

In my mind, I'm nearly panting. Panic begins to fill my veins, layering up little by little, like soot in a fireplace. Anxiety rattles in my chest, potent. I grip the iced tea Shell sets in front of me and take a long pull, focusing on the taste of the tea, letting it wash over my senses.

What did my sponsor, Rick, tell me to do?

Focus on the moment. On this one thing. Block out everything else. Breathe.

I inhale. Torsten asks for chips and guacamole. *Exhale.* Panda orders.

My nerves begin to settle. My heart rate slows. My vision clears.

"And for you?" Shell asks.

Panda and Torsten turn to me expectantly.

I clear my throat, passing my menu to Shell. "I'll take the veggie fajitas, please."

Torsten's shoulders relax and Panda throws me a grin. They think I'm fine. They don't know. No one does.

Inhale. Exhale. I lean back in my chair, feigning a hell of a lot more casual than I feel. Shell disappears. I lift my iced tea toward my teammates. "To you guys and the season." I smirk.

Panda and Torsten laugh. I watch as the cold beer touches their lips, as they swallow it down.

An inferno unleashes through my bloodstream, intense and furious, as I gulp back some iced tea. I close my eyes and force my thoughts to something else.

Claire fills my mind. Her golden hair, her dazzling eyes, her flirtatious wink. Clairebear.

She settles me, eases some of my anxiety. It's strange but deep down, I know she has my back. Even when she's not here.

I set down my iced tea. Relief floods my body as Shell drops off baskets with chips and guacamole and salsa.

I take a chip and pop it into my mouth.

Panda begins to talk about our upcoming game in St. Louis.

Little by little, I'm able to focus on the conversation, on Panda's assessment of our competition, on Torsten's take on this season. I'm able to be present in this moment with the beer bottles and the bar a persistent distraction but not an overwhelming thought in my mind, blocking out all others.

No, instead, I keep Claire at the forefront of my mind and she helps me get through this moment. Through my fear and uncertainty. Through my anxiety and anguish.

Today, Claire Merrick saves me.

BY THE TIME I walk through the front door of my brownstone, I'm nearly desperate to see her. I know the moment I do, a calmness will flood my body. I'm wired too tightly, nearly jittery with nerves and stress and feeling so fucking off-kilter.

I slam the front door closed.

"East? That you?" she calls from the kitchen and I'm so relieved that she's here, right now when I need her more than I ever have, that I stumble.

I drop my practice bag in the hall closet, kick off my boots, and hang up my coat. Gripping the sides of my head, I take a cleansing breath. Try to get some of my wild thoughts and frantic emotions under control.

I stride into the kitchen.

Claire looks up. She's seated at the kitchen island, her laptop in front of her, a cup of coffee by her elbow. Her hair is pulled back into a ponytail, an old sweater hanging off one of her shoulders.

"Hey," she says, frowning as she takes in my expression. "You okay?"

At the concern in her tone, I nearly break apart. How does she see everything I'm trying to hide like it's clear as day? How does she sense the turmoil rocking through me when the rest of the world smiles like I'm managing so well?

"Easton?" she asks hesitantly as I draw closer. "How was practice?"

I stop at the edge of the island, crossing my arms and leaning forward until my elbows hit the countertop. "Today was fucking hard, Claire," I blurt out the words in a rush. "It wrecked me. But I did it. And I'm so fucking happy to see you right now." I smile. This time, I mean it.

CHAPTER 10
CLAIRE

The moment I see his face, I know something is off. Lines bracket the sides of his mouth and his eyes are weary. For as long as I can remember, Easton Scotch has been all swagger.

But right now, he sways and I slip from the barstool.

My brow furrows as I search his eyes for an explanation. I don't understand the meaning behind his words but then he smiles the most brilliant, dazzling smile and my knees feel unsteady.

He's reaching for me. Right now, he needs solace, comfort, and understanding, and he trusts me.

The realization is a balm to the last year of Easton's dismissive remarks and rejections. I open my arms without hesitation and he falls into them. His hand cups the back of my head, cradling me against his chest in a surprisingly intimate hold. His fingers lace through my hair. His body wraps around mine protectively, even though the way his breath shudders makes it obvious that I'm holding him together.

The room spins as I pour my strength and compassion

into Easton. He clings to me with a vulnerability that's heartbreaking. I don't know how long we stand embracing but I could stay like this for eternity. The beating of East's heart sounds under my ear, the scent of him, cedar and sweat and need, lures me closer.

He shifts back slightly, peering down at me. The corner of his mouth pulls up in a smirk.

"You okay?"

He nods once, his blue eyes blazing. "Yeah."

"You want to talk about it?"

He tilts his head to the side, thinking. "Not really."

"But if you change your mind…"

He blows out an exhale and nods. His hand wraps around the end of my ponytail and he tugs. "Thanks for being here, Clairebear."

"East…" I shuffle back half a step. I don't want to push him, especially since he just alluded to not wanting to talk. But…

"Went out for lunch with Torsten and Panda." He frowns, scrubbing a hand over his face. "They ordered beers—"

I inhale sharply.

Easton's arm around my waist tightens. "No, they should. I mean, I want them to. I want to be able to go out with the guys on the team, with my friends, my brother, and not have them be weird about getting a Corona. But shit"—he shakes his head, his eyes tortured—"I hate that I can't control it. All of a sudden, I couldn't breathe, couldn't think."

"What'd the guys say?" I bite the corner of my mouth, hoping things aren't strained between him and his teammates now.

"Nothing," he half laughs. "I guess I hid it pretty well.

Ran through a bunch of these coping mechanisms, shit I learned in group therapy."

"Good. That's good, East." My hands wrap around his biceps. "I know this isn't easy but you're doing it. You're doing everything the right way because you're taking it all one day at a time. One situation at a time."

He scrapes his teeth over his lower lip. His eyes gleam and I swear the color in his cheeks heightens. "You know what I thought about to get me through the worst of it?"

I shake my head.

"You," he whispers. His eyes burn as they peer into mine, his nostrils flaring like he can't believe he admitted it aloud.

And me? I'm pretty much in a puddle on the floor because holyshitishefuckingkiddingme? "Really?" I ask, my tone way too hopeful to be chill.

East wraps his other arm around my waist, cradling me in his arms. "Really, Claire." He shifts his weight until his back is resting against the island. His eyes scan my face. They darken, navy and needy. "Shit."

"What?" I laugh nervously. My thighs clench together at the intensity in his expression, but he doesn't look away.

Instead he brings one hand up to rest on my cheek. The pad of his thumb draws a line down the center of my chin. His tongue darts out and swipes across his bottom lip.

I hold my breath. Hold it in my lungs as if my body knows that this moment is somehow going to change everything.

His eyes flare with an edge of concern and worry fans in my stomach. I press my cheek harder into his hold. "I knew I couldn't do this with you, Claire. That's why I didn't want you to move in."

"What are you talking about?" I watch his face, suddenly nervous.

"This." His thumb brushes over my cheekbone. "You being here, with your fucking energy and light and happiness."

"You want me to be moody and pissy?"

He snorts and shakes his head. "No, I want to not want to drag you up to your toes and kiss your mouth."

I gasp.

"See?" He grins at me but it's sinister. "I knew this would happen. I'm fucked up, Claire. I'm fucked up and you're sweet. I treat you like shit for a week and you cook me my favorite meal on one of my toughest days. I push you away and you pull me in." He takes my chin firmly, angling my head to meet his glare. "Why the hell do you do that?"

As Easton continues to ask questions, aka the best secrets my heart has ever heard, I close the distance between us. He needs me. He wants me. He's just too scared to do something about it.

But for him to let me in today, to tell me that I helped him get through the fog that clouded his mind at lunch, means something. I lean closer, a whisper of space between us. My chest heaves, each inhale dragging my breasts across the front of his shirt. I raise my arms but he catches my wrist in his large hand. Tension flares between us and electricity crackles. The pad of his thumb presses against my pulse. His bravado from a second ago has disappeared and now, he turns tortured, hungry eyes on me. "What're you doing to me, kid?"

I bite my lip, staring back. Kid. "Why do you call me *kid*? I'm not *that* immature?"

The corner of his mouth lifts in an almost-smirk. "To remind myself that you're too fucking pure for my world."

"That's what you think?" Frustration and a thrill flicker down my spine. Kid. It's not an insult as much as it's his last line of defense against…me. "Easton, I've, I've thought of you—"

His brow furrows.

"Thought of this—" I try to get my words out.

"Claire." His tone holds an edge of warning.

But I'm done playing games. Easton was right. He pushes and I reel him back in. Today, he said all the things I've been waiting years to hear. There's no way I'm going to let him dash it all by shoving me away right now. Nerves flicker through my body like a live wire. Years of wondering, hoping, dreaming and now here we are. Easton's touch at my wrist, his eyes locked on mine, emboldens me to slide my other palm up his arm and around his shoulder. I push up onto my tippy toes, and stare straight at him, allowing him to see all the things I want with him.

"Fuck," he murmurs, his eyes dropping closed as his head lowers. "Claire." His hands find my hips, his fingers digging into the flesh there. "You're Austin's sister."

"You're Noah's brother."

He snorts. "That's not the same thing, babe."

I shrug, my fingertips dusting over the tops of his shoulders. Even his shoulders are sexy.

"I've got nothing to offer you, Claire."

"I'm not asking for anything, East."

"But you deserve the world," he argues with me.

I pull back slightly. Who the hell is this man who is suddenly being so honest about his feelings? Let me revise —about his feelings for *me*? "I'll decide what I deserve," I whisper before I tug on his shoulders. Slowly, he lowers his face to mine and our lips finally—finally!—meet.

Easton Scotch's lips taste even better than I've spent an eternity imagining. Soft and full, his mouth molds to mine, pecking and nipping. His hands grip my hips as he tugs me closer and I go, gladly. He shifts back onto a barstool and drags me with him, until I'm straddling his lap, my knees braced against his outer thighs. As I sink down onto his lap and rock forward, he groans, his mouth moving harder, hungrier. I wrap my arms around his neck and part my lips just in time for his tongue to dip into my mouth and taste.

My eyes flutter closed as I turn off my head and just feel. This is the moment I've dreamt of for years. Easton Scotch is the man I've compared every single guy to, and now, right now, he's kissing me both sweetly and savagely, like I'm his salvation and his curse.

He tastes like mint and man, he smells divine, sweet sweat and hard work, and he feels like perfection under my touch. I bite down on his bottom lip and Easton moans, kissing me fiercely. I whimper into his mouth, my hands tracking his shoulders, down his back. I reach for the hem of his T-shirt and start to slide it up his body, the muscles around his ribcage rippling. Easton grows hard beneath me and I nearly see stars as I shift and rock against him, wanting him to undress me, and lay me out right here on the kitchen island.

"Fuck!" He rips his mouth from mine, his hands clamping down hard on my hips, holding me in place.

My eyes flicker open and take in the wildness of his. The slightest stubble shadows his jawline and I bite my bottom lip. Easton zeros in on the movement and his eyes shudder closed, an expression too similar to shame for my liking, washes over his features.

"Claire." He clears his throat.

Shit. He didn't mean to kiss me back. He wants to kiss me but doesn't want to want to kiss me and I just made things hella complicated between us. I slide backward to jump off his lap but his hands wrap around the backs of my thighs, holding me in place.

"Look at me." His voice is rough.

Slowly, I drag my eyes to his. My heart is racing and my stomach twists into knots. Did I just ruin everything between us? Will Easton go back to giving me the cold shoulder and dismissing me?

"Claire," he murmurs, one hand reaching up to cup my cheek. "Did you not hear anything I said?"

Huh? "About light and energy?"

He smiles, his face so beautiful I want to melt into it. "You're out of my league, babe."

I shake my head, my fingers toying with the collar of his T-shirt. "I've liked you for a long time, Easton."

He works a swallow, the hand still on the back of my thigh sliding up and down, just grazing the swell of my ass. "I'm no good for you, Claire."

"You don't know that," I say defensively. "All my life, everyone is always trying to tell me what to do. My parents, Vanny, Austin, even Indy. I know how I feel about you. I've known for a long time and you going to rehab didn't change that. Even if you've been a massive ass to me for the past year."

He winces, dropping my cheek to swipe a thumb over my lip. I nip at it and he pulls his hand away. "You're not a kid anymore, Claire."

"I haven't been for a long time."

"It was easier for me to pretend you were."

"It wasn't easy for me," I tell him the truth, hating that his rejection stung as sharply as it did.

"I never meant to hurt your feelings, bear." His hand catches the ends of my hair and tugs until I meet his gaze.

I smirk, shifting forward until our mouths are lined up once more. "I know how you can make it up to me."

Easton drops his head back and laughs. The sound is loud and uninhibited. It's music, the best damn melody I've ever heard.

He shakes his head and presses one hard peck against my mouth. Then, he taps my ass and I shimmy off of him. "We've crossed a line tonight, Claire. And right now, it's the only one I can handle."

I peer up at him, noting the conflicting emotions warring in his expression.

"Okay," I agree, a teeny bit disappointed. Clearly, I'd rather kiss Easton for the rest of my days and hope that the kissing leads to…more than just kissing.

"Come on." He drops an arm around my shoulder and leads me toward the game room. "I'll even watch one of your reality-TV shows."

I snort and snuggle into his side. Watching TV isn't my number one pick but being wrapped up in Easton's arms is hardly a consolation prize.

CHAPTER 11
EASTON

The rest of the week is long. Hard. And tempting as fuck.

I knew the first time I tasted Claire, I'd never be satisfied.

It's partly why I resisted her for so damn long.

But now that I've kissed her sweet mouth, now that my palms have grazed the curves and dips of her body, I can't go back to pretending.

Dinner tonight is deliciously torturous, like foreplay. Each bite Claire takes of her focaccia bread has my eyes narrowing. The strands of spaghetti she sucks through her plump lips has my throat drying. And don't even get me started on the sounds.

The girl eats with gusto, groans and sighs dropping from her mouth, as she revels in the tastes of our Italian takeout.

The only thing I'm grateful for is the lack of wine because I'm already beside myself.

"I'll clean up," I tell her as soon as she finishes.

"That's okay. I got it." She stands from the table and

piles our plates and utensils.

As Claire turns toward the sink, my gaze drops to her ass. Round, firm, and fucking perfect, I want to run my palms along her backside, grip her hips, and plunge into—

"Dessert?" She glances at me over her shoulder.

My gaze snaps up to hers.

Get a fucking grip, Scotch. What is wrong with you? This is Claire, not some random puck bunny.

"I made brownies this afternoon," she adds.

I close my eyes. Of course she did. On top of being perfect, she bakes. Three years ago, if I knew what I know now, I never would have lived with my brother. He never made dinner or brownies or looked like a ray of sunshine when I walked through the door.

"East?"

I clear my throat. "I'd love one. You know, you don't have to do all this." I gesture around the table. "I know you're pretty much here to babysit me, but you don't have to cook for me and pick up after me."

She rolls her eyes. "I made the brownies for myself. I'm only offering to share because I heard you missed three shots on goal today." She strides back toward the sink, the seductive sashay of her hips calling to me even as a burst of laughter breaks from my lips.

"You heard wrong!" I call after her, relieved that she manages to break all the tension with her flirty mouth and humor every damn time.

"That's not what my brother says. Or Big Daddy."

"Torsten?" I frown. "When did you talk to him?"

Claire comes back into view, setting down a plate with four brownies. She slides into the chair across from mine. "Earlier today."

I swipe a brownie from the plate and stare at Claire. Why the hell did my good time mood just swing wildly toward pissed-off? Torsten is cool with everyone. He's the biggest flirt on the planet but never has a girlfriend. Everyone knows this and yet…"Do you talk to him often?" I take a huge bite of brownie.

Claire pauses, watching me as I chew the delicious, fudge-like, chocolate goodness. "Are they good?"

"Are you kidding me?" I practically growl, shoving the other half in my mouth. "These are the best brownies I've ever had." Crumbs fall from my mouth and I don't even care.

Claire can cook *and* bake.

She visibly relaxes and bites into a brownie as I take up a second one. "You didn't answer my question."

She shrugs. "I talk to him every now and then. He needed help with something so he reached out, we chatted for a bit."

Huh? I lean back in my chair, considering this. *What does Torsten need help with? Why would he reach out to Claire?* "Do all the guys hit you up for advice or whatever?"

Claire swipes her tongue along her bottom lip to catch a brownie crumb. "Sometimes. I'm friendly with all of them. The team's unofficial little—"

"Sister," I finish, wincing. If I hook up with Claire, things won't just go south with Austin but with the entire team. I sigh. "Claire—"

"No." She holds up a hand.

"No what?"

"No, I'm not doing this with you. I am an adult, Easton. I've made it perfectly clear how I feel about you. And you've been honest with me too. Right?"

I nod, clearing my throat. For some reason, I feel like Clairebear, the girl I teased for being a kid for too many years, is about to school me. It's unsettling and I shift in my chair.

"We shared a kiss. One kiss." Her voice is forceful and I'm ashamed that she can talk about this a hell of a lot easier than I can.

"I know. It's just that, I don't want to mess things up between us, Claire. And it's not just us. Your brother is my best friend. The team is all I've got besides Noah. I can't—"

"Risk it all on me," she completes my sentence, softly.

Instantly, I feel like a giant ass. Especially at the look of dejection that fills her face. "It's not that either, babe."

She glances up, her eyes wary. "It's not?"

I place my brownie down and lean forward, closer to her. "It's not you, Clairebear. It's me. And that's not me feeding you some bullshit line either," I tack on when I get a read of her expression. "I'm out of rehab just over a month. I'm trying to stick to my routine, my schedule, my meetings. The support of the team, of your family, of *you*" —I pause, trying to find the right words—"I need it all, need you, more than I thought I would."

Across from me, Claire softens. She reaches across the table and laces my fingers with hers. The gesture is so simple and yet, when her thumb presses into my palm, it fills me with a silent strength I yearn for. "I want you, Claire. I want you in every way imaginable. But I can't lose everything, including you, when this goes sideways between us."

"Why would it go sideways?" Her voice catches and I hate the uncertainty I always manage to fill her with.

"Because I'm a fuckup, babe. And I will fuck this up. It's only a matter of time."

She shakes her head, her eyes as clear as a summer sky. "I don't believe that."

I chuckle harshly and move to lean back in my chair.

Claire catches my fingers before they can slide from her

grasp. She tugs me back and shakes her head. "Your problem is that you've always gotten away with everything."

"What do you mean?"

"No one's ever given you something to really believe in before. If you messed up, the only consequences were for you to bear. I'm not saying it didn't cut Noah or hurt members of your team, but this is different." She scrapes her teeth along her bottom lip and suddenly, I want to crawl across the table just to be closer to her.

What is wrong with me? What am I thinking?

"If you take me to your bed, Easton, you can't just walk away from me."

"I know that," I say, a strange mixture of anger and relief clogging my throat. At least she's finally seeing my point.

"So don't," she throws out, her eyes flaring with challenge.

"Don't what?"

"Don't mess it up. I dare you."

Is she kidding me right now? My mouth drops open but no sound comes out. Claire's resolve is obvious, her fingers tightening on mine.

"Claire, I can't just—"

"You've always been a risk taker, Easton. A gambler."

I blow out a breath, not refuting her statement. Because it's the truth. I take big risks, willing to lose it all, for that one moment of having it all. "I won't risk you, Claire."

She smirks. "Then don't lose." With those words, Claire drops my hand and stands from her seat.

I watch, hypnotized, as she rounds the table and comes closer to me.

"Claire," I warn, my ability to keep my hands to myself

nonexistent after trying to rein in my desperate thoughts for the past month.

Claire grins, her eyes flickering with the tiniest hint of vulnerability.

Fuck, I can't hurt this girl. *I can't.*

She doesn't stop walking until she's perched in my goddamn lap. The weight of her on my thighs feels better than it should. Instinctively, my fingers grip her waist, holding her closer when I should be holding her back. She winds her arms around my neck, her elbows hooked over my shoulders. We're eye level when she wets her bottom lip and my gaze drops to her mouth.

She smells like summertime and flowers, inviting and sweet. Her presence wraps around me and holds me captive. I don't stand a goddamn chance. There's no way I could reject what Claire is offering.

Because she's offering herself. More than just her body. But her care, her concern, her fucking light. Only a fool would deny her and I've been a fool ten times over. I won't turn her down again. I won't let her look at me with hurt when she could look at me with pride.

She believes I can do this. She thinks I can be strong enough to be worthy of her.

How can I let her down? How can I not even try? For her?

I lean forward slowly, closing the distance between our mouths. Claire inhales sharply, her eyes darting to mine before falling to my lips. My palm anchors the center of her back, my pinkie and thumb nearly grazing her ribs.

I breathe her in, savor this moment, allow myself to fall into its sweet promise. My lips touch hers softly, reverently, with an edge of hunger. I kiss her once, twice, and then I hold her close, until her breasts press into my chest and we're flush together. On the third kiss, Claire's lips part and my tongue eases inside, flicking against the tip of hers.

She sighs and lowers even more on my lap. My dick stirs as want races through my veins. I kiss Claire thoroughly, our need for each other escalating with each meeting of our tongues. I harden beneath the seam of her jeans. Her fingers clutch at the blades of my shoulders. When we're both breathing heavily, she grinds against me and I see stars, feeling more like a seventeen-year-old punk than a nearly thirty-year-old man that has had my fair share of women.

But none of them ever made me feel as clumsy and desperate as Claire.

I stand from the chair, lifting her in my arms, and stride toward the stairs. "What is it with you and chairs?" I whisper against her cheek as I press kisses down the column of her neck.

She giggles, breathless. "I gotta take what I can get when it comes to you."

I snort, taking the stairs two at a time. I enter my bedroom and toss her into the center of my bed. She looks relaxed and at ease as she scoots toward the headboard and props her back against the pillows.

I pull off my T-shirt and drop it to the floor, smirking as Claire's eyes drop—and linger—on my abs.

"What if I said I was going to give you everything, Claire?" I taunt, moving closer to the bed.

She gasps, her eyes flashing up to mine. "I'd say you better get to work, East."

His nostrils flare and his abs ripple at my words. Easton's tattoo, a colorful, elaborate, tribal-inspired design that treks up the left side of his ribcage captivates me. He clears his throat and I drag my eyes to his. Easton's eyes are dark and swirling—a hurricane about to unleash a torrent of wind and rain—and I am here for it. Nerves jumble in my limbs, packing together and unraveling like a spool of thread. I feel uncentered and excited and breathless.

Anticipation rocks through me, heightening my senses so I drink in each detail as it unfolds.

The scent of Easton's cologne mixed with fresh soap as it rolls off his pillowcase. The fading beams of sunlight displayed along his bedroom wall like a light show. The prowess in Easton's body as he strides forward. His expression both possessive and vulnerable. There's enough emotion in his eyes for me to drown myself in and I want to, willingly.

I've waited years for this moment, dreamed of this exact encounter, and now, it's finally happening.

My body hums approvingly as Easton crawls over my frame. His skin is hot where it presses into mine, his hands are rough, with calloused fingers and blunt fingernails, as they trail my skin. Exploring, touching, feeling.

I lie back against his pillows and revel in the feel of his weight as it drops over me. His hands brush my hair away from my face. For a long pause, we stare into each other's eyes, the way lovers might, even though we don't yet hold that title. His gaze is searching as it bores into mine, a probing glance to overturn secrets and unravel riddles.

"Claire," he whispers, his tone rough.

"I want you, East," I reassure him.

He sighs, closing his eyes for a long beat. His shoulders bunch and his body tightens. He's a man at war with himself, and for a moment, I let him battle. Because with each of my exhales, his body lowers over mine, and his resolve to keep fighting against this weakens.

"I don't want to hurt you," he admits on a hushed breath.

"Then don't," I murmur.

His eyes flash up to mine, the cocky grin I love rippling over his mouth. "It's that easy, huh?"

"It is if you want it to be."

"This feels like one hell of a risk," he mutters, his mouth arcing toward mine.

"Bigger reward," I manage to say before he kisses me.

Easton's kiss is like a drug and I am already an addict. He kisses skillfully, like a man with a lot of experience, but there's a hunger to his kiss. A desperate pressure to his mouth, a plea to his lips as they coax mine into submission. He kisses me like I'm his future and this is goodbye all at the same time.

I moan as he settles more firmly between my thighs. His hands clasp around my wrists, bringing them over my head and pinning them to the pillows. In this position, each inhale brings my breasts dragging across his chest. My breasts feel heavy, my nipples tingling, and I want nothing more than for him to undress me.

He doesn't disappoint. When his lips meet mine again, his control snaps. He kisses me fiercely, with a desperate hunger. I meet him kiss for kiss, our teeth clicking, our tongues dueling, our lips desperate for the upper hand. Easton has my shirt over my head and my bra popped open in a matter of seconds. We both shimmy out of our pants, our discarded clothes falling to the floor.

His eyes bore into mine, hazy with lust. "I'm going to ruin you for any other man, Claire. There won't be another fucking *Derek*." He spits his name, his shoulders trembling with a possessiveness that turns me on.

"Is that a promise?" I taunt.

Easton growls and pounces. I chuckle as his body covers mine once more, his hands touching every inch of my skin. "A warning, baby," he murmurs in my ear right before his fingers scrape against the scrap of lace between my thighs. He strokes my core and I moan. He does it again.

"Easton," I cry out, my back arching off the mattress.

Jesus, it's been too long. With all of my sassy talk and flirty banter, I haven't been with many men. Most of the time, I hold myself back. Something never feels right, but this, right now, feels too right to be anything else.

"You're so wet for me, Claire," Easton groans.

He shifts onto his side so he can watch my expression as he pleasures me like it's something he does every day.

"Don't be embarrassed," he murmurs, noting the heat on my cheeks. "Watching you come apart in my hands is magic."

I close my eyes as pressure builds low in my belly. Easton's lips streak across my chest and he clamps down on my left nipple just before he dips two fingers inside of me and curls them.

I nearly buck off the bed.

"That's it, baby. Give me everything," he demands, the stubble of his chin scraping up my throat until his mouth claims mine.

Between the assault of Easton's lips and the feel of his fingers inside of me, I reach the peak faster than I ever have before.

"East," I say, wonder and a hint of worry in my tone.

"Shh, I got you, Claire. Let me see you come for me."

My orgasm rips through me, as powerful as a tidal wave, as I break apart in Easton's arms. His fingers are relentless, his lips hungry. Ribbon after ribbon of pleasure bursts through my body, colorful and fragmented like a kaleidoscope of possibility.

I'm barely getting my bearings when my eyes pop open.

A million thoughts—*did Easton just make me come? Oh my God, what do I say?*—scramble in my mind. Before I can say anything, Easton sucks his fingers into his mouth and drags them out with a loud smacking sound.

"You taste better than dessert, Claire," he says, moving down my body like a freaking panther. All stealth and deliberate-like. My brows furrow together as I watch him. When he settles at the apex of my thighs, understanding dawns and I sit up.

"No, wait. Easton, I can't. You can't—"

He shakes his head and hooks my right thigh over his shoulder. "I can, Claire." He blows against my sensitive flesh and my thighs quiver. East grins saucily, his eyes meeting mine as his tongue darts out and licks a path straight up my center.

I cry out, flopping back against the pillows, my fingers twisting the duvet cover.

I moan as Easton does it again. His fingers hold my thighs open as he swirls his tongue over the little nub that drives me wild. I whimper and feel his chuckles vibrate against me. He works me over again until I'm seeing stars.

Another orgasm rocks through me, more powerful and intense than the first. "You're right," I wheeze out.

"About what, baby?"

"You've ruined me for any other man."

Easton snickers, flipping me over and lining up behind me. He pauses to unroll a condom. His hand runs over the swell of my ass. "Just getting started, Claire." Then, he pushes into me and the Earth tilts on its axis.

CHAPTER 13
EASTON

Heaven. Being inside of Claire is like owning a piece of heaven.

I'm desperate for her. Fucking delirious.

Pleasuring her was ecstasy. I loved seeing the flush build from her chest to her cheeks. I savored every moan that fell from her mouth, knowing I was responsible for it. And I fucking reveled in every orgasm I helped her achieve.

But right now, I'm balls deep inside of her tight body and I can't see straight. The only thing I can focus on is making this last as long as possible. I pull out slowly before plunging back inside of her, swearing.

She chuckles, shifting her weight so her ass pops even higher in the air. And God, the image of her like this is one that will stay etched on my eyelids for eternity. I work a rhythm between us, reveling in every gasp and groan that drops from her lips. My hands grip her hips savagely as I thrust into her, over and over. Her breasts swing from the momentum and I lean forward, removing one of my hands from her hips so I can fondle her breast. Jesus, I can't get enough of her.

Will I ever have my fill?

I tweak her nipple and increase my pace, drowning in the frantic panting of her breathing. It's a valiant effort but too fucking soon, my body coils and snaps, and I spill inside of Claire, hugging her to my chest and rolling us both to my mattress.

I hold her for a long moment, our heavy breathing the only sound in the room. I soften inside of her, slip out, and drag myself to the bathroom to clean up. Fuck, what the hell was that? Besides being the most intense sexual encounter of my life—which is saying something—it was with *Claire*.

I'm the last guy on the planet who wants to talk after sex but right now, that's exactly what I think Claire and I need to do. Except when I reenter my bedroom, her soft snores pierce the air.

I chuckle, watching her curled up on her side, her hands folded beneath her cheek. She looks like an angel. I pull the duvet over her sleeping body and crawl into bed beside her. Within moments, I pass out. For the first time in months, I dream of nothing.

When I wake in the morning, my body is pressed against Claire's and I'm already hard, ready for round two. Shit.

I peer at Claire, still sleeping beside me. The morning light filters through the windows, flickering shadows on the walls. Logically, I know I should be paralyzed with fear. Claire and I crossed every line, broke every rule, obliterated any possibility of being *just friends* last night. But I don't regret any of it. In fact, every second with her was worth it.

I brush my fingers through her hair.

I know I'm not good enough for her. She deserves a million times more than what I can offer. She deserves a man who is whole. Not one tormented by a monster. Not one who can barely see a beer without his throat closing. Not one who is a skilled liar, a deft con artist, a fucking shadow.

But now that I've had her, I can't walk away. Deep down, I know it and I hate myself for it.

The only solution is to be enough for her. Not what she deserves but enough of what she wants.

One month ago, I was safe, my conscience clear. It was easier to hold Claire off with insults and the cold shoulder. But now, I can't go back and the uncertainty that clogs my throat is nothing like the usual morning-after need to disappear, but an entirely different type of worry.

Claire Merrick could own my soul. And the darkest part of me desperately wants her to.

I blow out a shaky breath and watch as Claire stirs next to me. Her eyelids open slowly, heavy with sleep. When she spots me, a smile stretches over her face and the look of it, of her smiling for me, fills my chest with gratification. "Morning, Clairebear."

She stretches for me, her arms twisting around my neck. "Good morning."

"How'd you sleep?" I ask, my fingers toying with the sheet that covers her bare breasts. It slips a little and I catch a glimpse of her dusty rose nipple.

"Deeply," she murmurs. My head snaps up at her word choice. "I had the strangest dream…"

I grin, loving this sassy side of her. Of course, I always knew Claire as a little hellion, but Claire challenging me last night was more than I bargained for.

"Tell me about it," I taunt, running my nose along her jawline.

She purses her lips, pondering my question. Then she shifts, the heat of her skin gravitating toward mine. Her fingers press against my shoulders until I lie back against the pillows. She sits up straight and the sheet pools to her waist. Her breasts are perfect. The perfect size for my palms, the perfect weight against my fingers, just perfect. She swings a leg over my body and straddles my waist.

"What are you doing, babe?" I whisper, feeling my dick quicken to life as she sinks down.

"I'd rather show you," she whispers. Then she drops her mouth to my neck and trails open-mouthed kisses down my chest and abdomen. Her hands explore the planes of my body while her mouth tastes my skin greedily.

I try to stay still as she explores, but need coils in my veins. Between last night and now this, I'm desperate to claim Claire as mine and only mine.

She moves lower and lower as my limbs stiffen. She spends several long seconds studying, touching, kissing my tattoo. I reach for her, my fingers twisting in her hair. "Claire," I warn.

Then, I feel her tongue dart out and lick along the head of my dick. I inhale sharply, swearing, as I sit up.

She shakes her head, keeping her gaze trained on mine as she slowly drags her tongue up my shaft. "It's my turn to play, Easton," she says, pushing me back down.

I laugh, in awe and a little in love with this new glimpse of Claire. I feel drunk off her, intoxicated by her touch, delirious from her words. I lie back and watch as Claire takes me into her mouth. She pulls me in deeply and I swear as I hit the back of her throat.

She sucks me off expertly, and for a second, I wonder how the hell she learned to do this so well. A silent rage fills me at the thought of her doing this with other men, at the realization that other men have seen her the way I am right now. With plush lips, wild eyes, and a sexy body that is begging to be worked over.

"Fuck," I growl, pulling myself from her mouth. I move quickly to flip her over and slide on top of her. "Want you, Claire. Now."

In response, she surprises me again by widening her thighs. "Then take me, Easton."

"Jesus," I moan, my body trembling for hers. I'm so close to release, I try to stall and think awful things, just to make this moment last longer. "I'm clean, Claire."

"So am I. And I'm on the pill," she adds, giving me a knowing glance.

I rear back, surprised. It's quickly replaced by the grave understanding of how much trust she's placing in me. Claire Merrick's faith in me is its own type of drug, more powerful than liquor.

I brush her hair back and peer into her bottomless baby blues. "You sure, Claire? Because this changes everything."

She regards me for a long moment before offering a small nod. "Last night already changed everything, East. I know what I want."

I hold her gaze as I slide into her, inch by inch, watching as a myriad of emotions flit across her expression. Desire, vulnerability, excitement, a bloom of shock, a hint of need, and then something I can't place but it shines from her eyes like moonbeams.

When I'm all the way in, I still. She clutches at my shoulders and I press a desperate kiss to her lips. Then, I begin to move, finding a rhythm that has Claire moaning and me screwing my eyes closed to make this last as long as I can.

At the same time, we cry out, clinging to each other

with a recklessness that defies all logic, with a chemistry that burns all reason to ash.

"ACT NORMAL," Claire reminds me as we take the stairs up to her parents' front door.

"I'm always normal. It's you who's a loose cannon," I remind her.

She grins and hip checks me.

I smile back.

The door swing opens before we reach it and we both school our expressions.

"What's so funny?" Austin asks, peering at us.

Claire rolls her eyes and pushes inside, lifting up on her toes to brush a kiss across her brother's cheek. "Easton thinking he's got jokes," she replies breezily.

I'm impressed by her acting, and a strange jolt of possessiveness and delight grips me.

I watch as she disappears into her parents' kitchen before I step forward. When I look up, Austin is watching me curiously.

"What?" I ask, holding out a hand to shake hello.

"What's with you two?" he asks, his brow furrowing.

"Nothing, man. Claire's still a pain in the ass."

At that, Austin looks in the direction his sister disappeared, smiling affectionately. "She is that. Come on in, man. How are you doing?"

I step inside and Austin closes the door behind me. While I slip out of my winter coat and hang it in the hall closet, I respond, "Yeah, I'm good, thanks. Taking things day by day."

"You're looking good on the ice, East. I feel like we're all starting to gel again."

"Yeah. I feel good too. Better, I mean. But Sims has been doing a hell of a job."

Austin regards me strangely for a second before nodding. "Yeah, he has."

"Is that you, Easton?" Mary calls out from the kitchen. "I hope you brought your appetite."

"You know I did, Mary." I step into the kitchen and breathe in deeply. "Something smells delicious."

"Oh!" Mary laughs, coming over to kiss my cheek hello. "I made your favorite. I know you recently had chicken piccata, but I wasn't sure if Claire managed to pull it off. Since she never called me to talk about it..." Mary lets her unasked question hang in the air.

"It was the best he ever had!" Claire calls out.

I cringe at her word choice, but Mary bursts into laughter. Joe chuckles as he pours out glasses of Coke.

"Oh, you don't have to do that. You guys can enjoy your wine and beer." I hold a hand up to stop Joe, knowing the family always enjoys wine at Sunday dinners.

Joe stills, shooting me a serious look. "You sure, son?"

"Positive," I respond, my gaze darting to Claire who looks back with acknowledgment in her expression. "I went out to lunch with Torsten and Panda the other day too. I need to ease back into real life and this is the best place for me to do it." I gesture to the kitchen.

Mary's expression softens as she nods slowly. "You'll let us know if it's too soon? Too much?"

"I'd rather practice here," I admit. I turn and note Austin's strange expression again. "What?"

"Wait, I'm still on the part where Claire cooked you chicken piccata."

I chuckle. "It was good."

Austin's brows furrow until they nearly meet over his nose. "Are you sure she didn't poison you?"

Joe throws his head back and laughs.

"Oh come on now," Mary says indulgently, taking out a bottle of wine. "Claire does a wonderful job."

"Oh, now you stick up for me." Claire slips beside Mary and snakes an arm around her waist. "What happened to 'I wasn't sure if Claire managed to pull it off'?'"

Mary blushes and Joe's laughter grows.

Austin snickers and he shakes his head. "She totally poisoned you." He points at me. "You're being way too nice to her."

A knock sounds on the door and Mary claps her hands together. "That must be Jemmy and Leanne."

"Or Noah and Indy," Austin supplies, heading for the door. "I'll get it."

Claire sticks her tongue out at his back and Joe chuckles, tugging on her ponytail.

I slide onto a barstool and clutch my glass of soda, relaxing as I watch the Merrick family antics unfold. It feels like home.

CHAPTER 14
CLAIRE

"You're blushing." Rielle smirks at me before lifting her caramel macchiato to her lips and taking a long sip.

"Isn't it wonderful?" Indy sighs, clasping her hands to her chest.

"You've gotten so gushy since Scotch put a baby in you," I tell my cousin, rolling my eyes. I swear, in a handful of months, my serious, Type-A, often boring cousin has transformed into the poster child for love. She could star on a dating website for the amount of hearts and stars that shine from her eyes.

"You're coming in at a close second," Rielle accuses me. "In all fairness, I've never seen you as twisted up over a man as Easton, but this tops the cake. The sex must be stellar."

I sigh, totally pulling an Indy. "It's orgasmic."

Rielle cracks a smile as Indy laughs.

"But it's more than that," I continue, leaning forward like I'm about to divulge a secret. "He made me breakfast," I whisper.

Rielle's mouth drops open and Indy gasps, clutching her chest again, this time in surprise.

"No way." Rielle points at me. "You're serious?"

I nod.

"Damn." Indy whistles. "That's like relationship level."

"I know, right?" I grin, picking up my latte. "I mean, I spent the morning blowing his mind so I needed nourishment but—"

Rielle bursts out laughing.

"I still didn't expect the omelet and whole wheat bagel and orange juice."

"What was in the omelet?" Indy narrows her eyes.

Rielle shoots her a look and I giggle. "It was a veggie omelet. Why?"

Indy shakes her head. "I'm just…surprised. Ever since we were teenagers, Easton rarely went out of his way to do anything nice for anyone."

"I know," I agree.

"It's definitely more than just sex," Rielle decides.

Even though I think it's more than just sex too—I mean, it *feels* like more than just sex—having Indy and Rielle confirm it makes it more real.

I beam at them like I won the lottery. Ten times over.

"Have you told anyone? I mean, anyone except us?" Rielle asks.

I shake my head. "Easton hasn't brought it up. I mean, we haven't talked about what we are or anything…"

"You're dating," Indy says with confidence.

"I guess so." I worry my bottom lip between my teeth.

"What is it?" Rielle asks.

"It's just, I think Easton is worried about what Austin and my parents will think. Plus, the team…"

"They do all treat you like their little sister," Indy agrees.

Rielle shakes her head. "I can't imagine having my own brother give a shit about who I date, never mind ten hulking hockey players."

Indy glances at her curiously but I give a subtle shake of my head to let my cousin know that Rielle's family is off-limits. She doesn't speak of her family often; in fact, she rarely brings them up. When she does, it's usually as an afterthought and any prodding on the subject—been there, done that—results in her clamming up completely.

Indy reaches across the table and grasps my wrist. "Claire, if you're this into East and things are going so great, you can talk to him, you know?"

"I know."

"I just don't want to see you hang out in relationship limbo because you're too scared to rock the boat. I did that with Noah and it sucks."

"I know," I say quietly, remembering the anguish that Indy's uncertain relationship status with Noah caused both of them just a few weeks ago. "But it's still new."

"True." Indy nods. "And you're not knocked up." She narrows her eyes. "Are you?"

I flip her the middle finger and she grins as Rielle snorts.

"It's different this time. Everything with Easton is just *different*." I can't stop the grin from splitting my face. "With him, I feel like I can do anything. I mean, he's so supportive of my designing band logos and encourages me to follow my dreams, to do something I'm passionate about. After months of having my parents and Austin on my case about finding a real job, it's just nice to have someone in my corner, you know?"

Rielle nods slowly, her gaze searching as it scans my face.

But Indy straight up frowns. "I had no idea you were so serious about the band logos."

I wince. "I am. I just, I was embarrassed to tell you."

"Why?" My cousin looks genuinely confounded, and guilt pierces my chest.

"Isn't it obvious?" I force a light laugh. "Indy, you're perfect."

"Straight up, you are," Rielle agrees.

Indy shakes her head. "No I'm not. I—"

"You're organized and disciplined," I cut her off.

"Focused and determined," Rielle adds.

"You know exactly what you want and go after it with tenacity," I tack on.

Rielle nods. "I wish I was as ambitious as you."

Indy's brow furrows as she looks between us. "But you're creative and passionate, Claire. And Rielle, I don't know anyone who works as hard as you."

"Because I have to," Rielle mutters, taking a large gulp of her beverage.

"And my creative and passionate side are dismissed." I fiddle with the handle of my mug, glancing at Indy. "My parents would think my dabbling in band logos is a cute hobby for my boredom."

Indy's shoulders slump and I watch as realization flickers over her expression. "I'm so sorry, Claire. I had no idea. If I had, I would have backed you up more. You know I support anything you want to do."

I nod. I know she's telling the truth. If I had been more vocal and upfront about what I wanted, Indy would have had my back. "It's just, it's nice that Easton noticed it without me having to say it."

"I understand that." Indy smiles at me. "Then I'm happy for you. And if you ever want to talk to someone for some perspective or help setting things up, you know Aiden is an entertainment lawyer, right?"

"Your best friend, Aiden?" I ask, recalling Indy's childhood bestie from Florida who spent Thanksgiving with us. "Didn't he just move here?"

"Yes. He arrived last week. You can sit and talk with him anytime you're ready."

I smile at Indy, a wave of gratitude rushing through me. "Thanks, Indy. I'm not really there yet but as soon as I am, I'll definitely take you up on that."

She waves her hand. "Anytime. And if you ever want someone to check out bands with, Aiden is definitely your guy."

"Cool, thanks." I smile.

"I'm happy you finally found the happy ending with East you were waiting for," Indy adds.

Rielle lifts her mug. "Cheers, baby girl. I'm happy you're so damn happy."

I smile and clink my mug against Indy's and Rielle's. But I don't miss the curious glance they exchange, or the worry that rings my best friend's eyes just before she drinks.

Shaking it off as they're being overly concerned, I dismiss it. Because I'm too happy for anyone to rain on my parade.

This morning, I woke up to Easton's head between my legs. And let me tell you something, there's no coming back from that. He's ruined me for any other man, but it doesn't matter, because there will be no one after Easton.

He's my future.

"MISSED YOU TODAY," East whispers. His lips brush across mine, rousing me from sleep.

Dreams still cloud my vision as I force my eyes open. "What time is it? I must have dozed off."

"Just after 6 p.m."

"Oh." I frown. "I can't believe I slept so long."

Easton smooths his thumb over my forehead. "It's my fault, babe. Been keeping you up too late."

I grin. "I like how we spend our time."

Easton chuckles and collapses next to me on the couch. He tugs me into his arms, our chests pressed together, as he kisses my nose. "You do, huh?"

I nod, snuggling deeper against him. "How was practice?"

East shrugs, uncertainty flickering over his face for an instant. In the next blink, it's gone. "It was okay."

I frown. "Do you want to talk about it?"

He shakes his head, grinning slyly. "Not when there are so many better things we can be doing."

My heart soars at the playful gleam in his eyes. He showers me with attention and affection, two things my soul has been starved for far too long. "What did you have in mind?" My voice is huskier than I intend and East bites the corner of his mouth, his eyes flashing.

He pulls me higher on his chest, until our lips are lined up. We inhale each other's exhales and it's surprisingly intimate. "I wasted too much time with you, Clairebear," he murmurs, kissing me slowly. The tip of his tongue traces the seam of my lips and as I part them, he pulls back. "Gotta make up for lost time." He grins before capturing my mouth again.

This time, there's spice behind his sweet. In moments, I'm pinned beneath him on the couch. Easton's tongue plunges into my mouth and I arch into him, desperate for more. Desperate for everything. His hands are rough as they trail up my ribs, dragging my shirt up. He rips his mouth from mine and clamps it over my right breast. My hands dart to his hair, pulling him closer as my legs encircle his waist.

"Need you," I practically whimper. Already, heat pools between my legs. How is it possible that with just a few kisses and touches, I'm desperate and needy? How does Easton elicit this type of reaction from my body in a matter of moments?

"You have me, Claire." He unclasps his belt and makes quick work of his jeans. His hair is still damp from his shower after practice. It curls around his ears; messy, making him look like the boy from our teenage years. But the look he gives me is all man, and I shiver from the intensity in his gaze.

Easton smells like soap and winter. He looks like the perfect combination of an Ancient Greek god and a modern Calvin Klein underwear model. He wrecks me with a simple glance, ruins me with his touch, and drowns me with his kiss.

As Easton unrolls my leggings and kisses up the length of my thighs, I drop my head back and close my eyes. The heat of his mouth causes my body to break out in goosebumps. His hand snakes up my stomach until his fingers close around my breasts, massaging erratically just as his tongue licks up my center.

I gasp. Easton blows lightly on my overly sensitive flesh. He pinches my nipple. "You're so fucking hot, Claire," he declares before lowering his mouth.

This time, he feasts on me like I'm Thanksgiving dinner. And I revel in every second of it.

After I shatter apart, he slides into me. We fit together perfectly. With our rhythm in sync, our gazes lock together and hold. All the words Easton struggles with pour from the heady look he gives me. All the things I need to hear press into my skin through his touch. He fills me up with wonder and hope. I chase away his demons.

The sounds of our bodies coming together fill the air, wrapping us in a cocoon sheltered from the rest of the world. As Easton's dark blue eyes bore into mine, I realize I don't need anyone to know about us. I don't need anyone but him. Nothing but this.

Because *this* is enough. In fact, it's everything.

CHAPTER 15
EASTON

Claire Merrick unravels me.

With each passing day, the burn in my throat, the ache in my mind, ease. Instead, I replace one addiction with another. Claire.

The taste of her skin. The feel of her curves. The scent of her hair.

The wit of her mind. The smirk of her mouth. The dazzle in her eyes.

Claire Merrick mesmerizes me. She provides a salvation after too many nights spent in hell.

It's easy for us to settle into a routine. I wake up wanting her, spend my day thinking about her, and close my eyes at night with the scent of her on my skin.

Desperate and lost in lust, it doesn't take long for Noah, Austin, and the other guys on the team to realize I'm twisted up over a woman.

But there's no way in hell I'll tell them it's Claire. At least, not until they force me to.

Because I don't want to share my slice of heaven. I don't want their expectations to taint the delicate thing we've got going on. Right now, Claire is the only bright spot in my life. And I'll damn anyone who dares to darken her light.

"Hey." Her smile greets me as she walks into the kitchen.

"Hey." I pull the plate of leftovers from the microwave and gesture to it. "You hungry?"

She shakes her head. "No way. We've got dinner at my parents' tonight and you know how Mom still force-feeds me."

I chuckle. Mary Merrick is a total food pusher. But, as a kid who grew up with a mother who couldn't care less if I ate or not, I appreciate Mary's commitment. "This will hold me over." I take a bite of the chicken parmigiana.

Claire scoots up onto a barstool and watches me eat. Every few seconds the heel of her shoe clangs against the bottom rung of the barstool.

"What's on your mind, bear?"

She looks up at me and shakes her head, as if to clear it. "Nothing."

"Ah, come on. I can practically hear the thoughts turning in your head. What's going on?"

She sighs and her fingers toy with the edge of her shirt sleeve. A trickle of unease drips down my throat, slowly filling my chest with worry. Did something happen? Does she not want to live here anymore? I hate the negative thoughts that fill my mind, but suddenly, I feel panicked at the thought of losing Claire.

"Claire?" I prod impatiently.

"Do you think, I mean…" She pauses. "Are you ashamed of me?"

"What?" I bark out a laugh. "Ashamed of you? Are you drunk?"

She rolls her eyes at me but a small smile plays over

her mouth. "It's just, you haven't told anyone about us. I mean, we haven't really talked about it. But Rielle and Indy know—"

"That we're..." I gesture between us.

She nods, her brow furrowing as she reads the uncertainty in my expression. Shit.

"You don't want people to know?" Her voice is small.

I shake my head, leaning over the island to hold her wrist. "It's not that, babe."

"Then what is it?"

"Look, Claire." I huff out a breath. The truth is, she's the only person in my life who has faith in me and while I revel in it, I know better than to believe it's true. "Baby, I'm trying. Every day, I do my goddamn best to do all the right things. To not slip up. To be good for you."

"I know that. And you are."

I grin at her. "Claire, you are the only person I know who has so much trust in me. And before you say it's not true, I know that it is. I need you, Claire. I need you a hell of a lot more than you need me."

"Easton..." She winces as if my words pain her but sometimes the truth *is* painful.

I tighten my hold on her. "If everyone knows we're hooking up—"

"Is that all this is?"

I sigh, amending my statement. "If everyone knows we're together—"

Her expression brightens and I grin.

"Well, then, there's another layer of expectations and I don't know if I'm ready to manage it all. There's Austin, your parents, hell, the whole team—who will point out that I'm too messed up for you. That we're not a good idea. My sponsor is already nervous that I jumped into things with you so quickly."

"Rick knows about us?"

I nod, wetting my lips. "Does that bother you?"

She shakes her head, her eyes wide. "Of course not. East, I just want what's best for you. That's all I've ever wanted."

"You're what's best for me, Claire. But I'm not what's best for you. And I'm too selfish to let you go the way I know I should."

"Don't you dare!" She pulls me closer until I'm hovering across the island. Grinning at me cheekily, she slides right onto the island and kisses me deeply.

Claire disarms me. How the hell will I survive her?

She pulls back suddenly and brushes her fingers over my mouth. "We don't have to tell anyone if it's too much. I just wanted to make sure we're on the same page."

"What page is that, babe?"

"The one where this is going somewhere."

I nod, reading the vulnerability in her gaze. "I'm not screwing around with you, Claire. I swear, I want this as much as you do. I just don't want to mess it up. We rushed into this a lot faster than I anticipated and now that we're here, I don't want to slow down, but sometimes I think we need to slow down. Do you know what I mean?"

She nods solemnly. Claire shifts her weight until she's hovering on the edge of the kitchen island. I step between her thighs, my chicken parmigiana forgotten. My hands settle on her upper thighs and I squeeze. "I don't want to lose you, Claire. It feels like we're constantly hovering on the edge of a cliff and one wrong move, something as simple as a breeze in the wrong direction, will knock us over," I admit, sharing my fear to the best of my ability. Part of me knows I'm going to lose her. How could I not? But a small flicker of hope keeps flaring in my chest.

What if I could be enough? What if I could take the biggest risk of all and love Claire the way she deserves?

"I won't let that happen," she declares confidently.

I grin at her brazenness, knowing if anyone could ward off Mother Nature or fate, it would be Claire.

Her expression grows earnest and she runs her hands up my arms, settling them on my shoulders. Looking directly into my eyes, she takes a deep breath. "I don't want to scare you, East. But I'm falling in love with you."

I freeze, my limbs locking down as I watch Claire's face. And God, she's fucking breathtaking.

"I have been for a long time," she continues. "I have all these *feelings* for you. Sometimes I don't even know what to do with them. But I hate thinking that I'm the only one feeling them all."

"You're not," I say quickly, wanting to put her at ease. My heart thumps so loudly, it rings in my eardrums. My palms grow clammy and a strange sense of elation mixed with dread swells in my chest. "Christ, Claire. I'm no good at this," I admit, raking a palm over my face. "I don't know how to talk about my feelings and shit. I was taught at a young age to keep it all locked down."

Claire frowns, her eyebrows dipping together. I never talk about my childhood, my past, and the monsters that lurk there. Why would I?

I shake my head to clear it of thoughts of my parents. "But baby, believe me when I tell you that you're not alone. I'm desperate for you, for all of you. And most days, I'm petrified of screwing it all up."

Her hands clasp the sides of my face as she pulls me toward her and kisses me softly.

My hands curl into fists and press into the unforgiving granite of the countertop as I cage her in and deepen the kiss. In moments, Claire's breathing is elevated. I continue to kiss her passionately, pressing into her space until she lies back on the countertop. I grasp her thighs and tug her to the edge.

She grins at me as I pull my shirt off and pop the button on her jeans.

"I'm no good with words, Claire."

"You did okay," she whispers.

I shake my head. "I'd rather show you." I lose my pants.

"Here?" Her eyes widen as she glances around the kitchen.

"Anywhere you'll let me." I settle back in between her thighs and dip my head to press kisses along the sliver of skin where her shirt rides up.

She shimmies out of her shirt while I pull her jeans off her shapely legs. Her eyes lock onto mine and goose-bumps rush over her skin as I peel off her underwear. Lust colors her gaze.

"You ready for me, baby?" I murmur, dragging two fingers down her center.

She whimpers.

I bring my fingers to my mouth and suck off her arousal, watching as her eyes cloud over.

"Sweet," I tell her truthfully. Gripping the back of her knee, I lift her leg, line up at her entrance, and push inside of her.

Her eyes roll back and I help her shift her weight until I can slide all the way inside. Claire grips at my forearms as I pull back before plunging deeper.

"Easton," she cries out.

"I got you, baby." I set a steady pace that quickly turns unrelenting as the thread holding me together snaps.

Claire Merrick, with all of her flirty banter and beauty,

unravels me. Her sweetness shreds me. Her sass schools me. But her fucking heart loves me.

And it's the only thought I need as I plow into her like I'll never be worthy enough. Like I might never have her again. Like every moment between us is precious.

For a washed-up hockey player who keeps falling off the wagon, I know it is. Nothing is promised. Nothing is forever. No matter how much I hope for it, no matter how much I wish to be enough for Claire, I'll always fall short of what she deserves.

I fuck her hard and she meets me thrust for thrust until we're both crying out, shattering at the exact same time.

I swear, falling forward and covering her body with mine.

"You destroy me, Claire," I breathe out raggedly.

She pants in my ear for several breaths. Her hand strokes my hair reassuringly. "I won't let you destroy us," she whispers with an understanding I desire and despise.

CHAPTER 16
CLAIRE

I adore living in Boston. I like the bustling city streets. I love the energy that permeates the city in spring. I enjoy the timelessness mixed with modernity in the architecture, the exhibits, and the restaurants. I don't even mind the traffic.

What I dislike is February. February in Boston is brutally cold. The kind of cold that seeps into your bones and makes your socks damp, even if there's no snow on the ground. The charm of autumn with her colorful leaves is dead, and the budding hope of spring has not yet sprung.

February in Boston makes loitering on the front steps of my parents' house with a hunky, hockey heartthrob impossible. So instead of continuing the flirty exchange that Easton initiated in the car, I dart up the steps and throw myself through the front door before I catch pneumonia.

Austin says I'm melodramatic but I'm just stating facts.

"Whoa!" Austin grips my shoulders as I plow into him. "You okay?" He leans back to peer down at me.

I grin at my brother and nod. "It's freezing out."

Austin snorts. "You live in the wrong city." He glances up as Easton crosses the threshold. "Hey East."

"What's going on, Aus?" East asks, slipping out of his coat. He hangs it in the hall closet before taking mine and hanging it next to his.

Is it lame that I like how our coats look hanging together? Yes, yes it is. But for a second, I can picture a lifetime of our coats hanging side by side. It's like having our toothbrushes chill together in the cup by the sink or our keys mingle on the little dish inside the front door.

Easton and I could build a whole life together and the realization that we're moving in that direction fills my soul with happiness.

"You sure you're okay?" Austin shakes my shoulder and I look at him.

When I realize I'm grinning like the Joker, I press my lips together and nod. Austin shoots me one more strange look before asking Easton a question about their upcoming game in Chicago.

I trail my brother and Easton to the kitchen where Mom has already prepared a spread on the kitchen island. Crackers, cheeses, Italian meats—my mom is the Queen of charcuterie boards, and we all bow down.

"Hey sweet girl." Mom kisses me hello.

"Hi, Mama." I hop up onto a barstool and help myself to some cheese and crackers. Dad sets a glass of wine down in front of me and I grin up at him. "How's it going, big guy?"

Dad chuckles, affectionately ruffling my hair. "It's going, short stack. What have you got going on?"

I take a sip of the wine and glance at Mom. "I see you opened the good stuff."

She snorts.

"What's going on?" I ask my parents.

Mom crosses her arms and leans forward on the island. "Just hear us out, okay?"

I nod slowly, taking another sip of wine.

"I saw John Kimber at the gym the other day," Dad starts.

I lift an eyebrow. "You're working out?"

"Don't get sidetracked, Claire," Mom warns.

I squeeze Dad's bicep for good measure and he swats my hand away.

"The wine is meant to lure me into a false state of calm, isn't it?" I lift the glass and swirl its contents around. "The limpidity is excellent."

Mom rolls her eyes.

I sigh. "Okay, ambush me. What's the job?"

Dad stares at me for a long moment, an expression I don't understand crossing his face. "We're just trying to help you, Claire."

I nod. Deep down, I know my parents' hearts are in the right place. But instead of encouraging me to search for the "steady and secure" job prospects, why can't they encourage me to seek out the "fulfilling and creative" opportunities?

"His son, Jacob, do you remember him?" Mom cuts in.

Jacob Kimber. He graduated two years before me and played Varsity baseball. He felt me up during a bonfire one Friday night after I pre-gamed a six-pack of Mike's Hard Lemonade with my friend Megan. It was the first time I ever drank and I was tipsy, giggly, and very unsure of myself. "I remember him."

"He's working in Chicago now at a marketing firm. He's done very well for himself," Dad explains, leaning back in the chair next to mine. "Worked his way up. That boy has always been a go-getter, ambitious, and dedicated."

I wrinkle my nose, briefly wondering if Dad would sing Jacob's praises if he knew how he snapped my bra and fondled my breasts even after I pushed his hands away and told him to stop. I smacked him when he shoved his hand down the back of my pants and told him I didn't feel well. He kept going until Megan "spilled" a beer on him.

"He needs an assistant." Mom drops the hammer.

I look up, alarmed. "An assistant?"

"Oh, Claire," Mom huffs, "don't be so dismissive before you hear him out."

"You want me to work *for* Jacob Kimber? Like, plan his schedule and bring him coffee?" My tone drips with disdain and I don't try to disguise it.

Dad narrows his eyes at me. "It's honest work, Claire. What are you doing now? Living rent-free in your brother's best friend's house and having Mom and I bankroll your life. Do you think that gives you a sense of entitlement to turn your nose up at being someone's assistant? It could kickstart your career in the right way, with the right company."

"Until there's a sexual harassment charge," I mutter.

Mom furrows her brows and Dad looks truly shocked.

"What are you talking about?" Austin cuts in.

Behind him, Easton's expression locks down. He curls his hands into fists and watches me with a controlled intensity that makes my skin tingle.

"Nothing," I say.

"Did something happen with Jacob Kimber?" Mom asks slowly.

I close my eyes and breathe out an exhale. This went sideways quickly. "It's nothing. Forget it."

"Claire." Dad's tone is firm. I make eye contact. "If there's something that happened—"

"It's not a big deal. I'll talk to him if you want."

Mom looks truly concerned. "Claire, we just want what's best for you. And I'm not saying that's Jacob Kimber," she adds quickly. "You have to meet us halfway, sweetheart. Help us understand the type of jobs you're applying for. What do you want to do, Claire?"

I bite my lip, holding back the torrent of words that dance on the tip of my tongue. Do I tell them the truth? That I've been earning steady money from my design work with indie bands. That an up-and-coming band out of New York just contacted me about designing their logo. That I'm moving on from logos and doing merchandise design and website branding as well.

Before I can decide what to say, Easton announces, "Claire's doing an incredible job designing band logos and album covers."

"Band logos?" Mom asks, surprised.

Dad's shoulders stiffen as his gaze swings to Easton and then back to me. He presses his lips together. "What kind of band logos? For who?"

"She was just contacted by a hot band out of New York," Easton says, leaning his hip against the kitchen island. "Her demand has really picked up over the last few weeks. Hell, if she made a real go at this, she could probably run her own empire instead of bringing some entitled prick who has clearly taken *liberties* with her his morning cappuccino."

"Jacob is more of an americano kind of guy," I throw out, unnerved by how quickly Easton jumped to my defense. My attempt at levity is ignored.

"Tell us about the band logos, Claire," Austin says, giving me a nod.

His encouragement eases some of the anxiety curling in my chest like rope. There's enough slack to hang myself but at Austin's nod and Easton's support, I take a deep breath.

"I started messing around with it for fun. Over the summer, I was seeing this guy—"

"What guy?" Dad frowns.

"A musician. He's, um, the lead singer for The Burnt Clovers."

"Derek Reiner?" My brother's mouth drops open.

Mom's brow furrows. "Should I know him?" she whispers.

I shake my head. "Anyway, I was just messing around and mocked up some logos for his band and the guys all loved one of them. It's actually the one they went with, and then they were invited on tour with The Failed Poets so—"

"They kept your logo?" Austin asks, sounding impressed.

I grin at him. "They did. I've also done some merch for them. Derek's introduced me to some other bands and, it sort of just happened. I'm now making teaser graphics for their social media accounts and website branding too. I've only done a handful of album covers but they're my favorite. I love brainstorming different concepts and working one-on-one with musicians to bring their visions to life." I shrug, staring into Mom and Dad's shocked expressions. "I really love it. And I'm good at it. It's not a ton of money now but I haven't really structured it to be. I think Easton's right though. If I made a real go of it, I do think I could turn it into a small business to support myself."

"Twenty-percent of businesses fail in their first year," Dad points out.

"Joe," Mom says.

"There's the support I was counting on." I move my arm in a gung-ho fist pump and Austin winces.

Dad glares at me. "I'm being realistic, Claire. You should too if this is something you're seriously considering. You have a college degree and a wide network of contacts at your disposal. Instead of tapping into them, you want to sit home, drink fancy Starbucks beverages, and design a band logo for a guy who only paints one of his fingernails black."

Mom gasps. Austin covers his snicker with a cough. I don't even look at Easton to see the laughter burning in his eyes.

"You know Derek?" I ask.

Dad glowers.

"Right now, he's feeling more of a navy tone. It's not so heavy for his image."

"Claire Josephine Merrick." Mom full-names me. It's a warning I should heed.

Dad scrapes his hand over his face. "You've always been difficult, Claire."

"Passionate," Mom amends.

I shoot her a grateful smile and turn back to my father. "Can't you just be happy for me? I'm doing something I love and I'm earning more money than interning for free."

He shakes his head, clearly at a loss. "Just promise me you'll keep applying for real jobs. You know, ones that will allow you to get a mortgage and have health insurance."

I bite back the snarky remark desperate to break free and nod. "Sure."

Austin tops off my wine glass and winks at me.

The doorbell rings, bringing a wave of relief to the kitchen. Mom and Dad both beeline to the door to welcome Aunt Leanne, Uncle Jemmy, Indy, and Noah inside.

The second they're gone, Austin, Easton, and I burst into laughter.

"Navy is lighter for his image?" Austin asks.

I smirk.

"You've got *cojones*, Claire," my brother adds.

"One of us in this family has to," I reply.

He flips me his middle finger. Easton walks around the island to stand beside me. He grips the back of my neck and squeezes. I look up at him and grin, momentarily blinded by his smile.

"Thank you," I whisper to him.

"You're so much bigger than you realize, Claire," he murmurs back, dropping his hand. Immediately, I miss the warmth of his touch.

I pick up my wine glass as Indy and Noah filter into the kitchen. Aunt Leanne and Uncle Jemmy's voices float behind them.

"Hey!" Indy kisses my cheek hello. "I talked to Aiden the other day and he's going to get in touch with you. He's checking out some new talent who may be looking for representation and said you're more than welcome to come with."

"Really?"

She nods. "Yeah. He's pretty pumped about this rapper, Big Roxi. I listened to some of his tracks and you'll definitely like his music. He also mentioned something about a bluegrass band."

I grin. "That sounds awesome. Thanks, Indy."

"Anytime. Honestly, you're doing Aiden a favor too. He loves being in the entertainment industry and I think checking out new artists is his favorite part. But since he's new to the city, he'd rather not go solo."

"Cool. I'll wait to hear from him then. Mom got non-alcoholic sparkling wine for you," I tell her, slipping down from my barstool. I move to pull the bottle out of the bar refrigerator but pause when I get a look at Austin's face.

My brother looks at me curiously. The wheels in his head are turning as his gaze darts to Easton and back to me. I stiffen immediately and duck into the bar fridge, grateful for the cold air that cools the heat of my cheeks.

After the showdown with Dad, the last thing I need is for Austin to discover just how much his best friend supports his little sister.

CHAPTER 17
EASTON

"You stuck up for me," she whispers in my ear after dinner.

I turn in my chair, hooking an arm around her so I can peer into her face. "I'll always stick up for you, babe. I'm proud of you."

She grins. Her eyes dart around the empty den. We finished dinner about half an hour ago. Indy and Claire helped Mary and Leanne clear off the table and prepare the dessert while Austin, Jemmy, Noah, Joe, and I retired in here to watch some hockey. There's a minor league game on tonight between Windsor and Toronto. But then Joe needed Jemmy's help with something, Indy called on Noah, and Austin snuck away to take a phone call.

In this moment, it's just Claire and me. Immediately, the atmosphere eases and I relax into the armchair I'm sitting in. Claire always puts me at ease. Since leaving rehab, she's the only person I can fully relax around and I crave her presence. I tug on her hand and she perches on my knee. I breathe in her floral, flirty perfume, and run my fingertips over the smooth skin that exists between the bottom of her sweater and the waistband of her jeans.

She drops her head to my ear. "Want to sneak away with me?"

I grin at the suggestion in her tone. "Where would we go?"

She slips off my lap and holds out a hand. "I'll show you."

I snort, shaking my head. Voices from the kitchen float into the den. "We're at your parents' house, Claire."

"I know."

I smile at the dare in her eyes. They shimmer brightly, blue like sapphires. "You better hurry up, Scotch. I thought you liked to play with fire."

I stand from my chair and grip her hand. "You thought right, babe."

She giggles and pulls me through the den and down the hallway. Pausing at the end of the hall, she looks both ways and I fight the urge to laugh. She's so fucking cute. Everything with Claire is fun and playful, real and raw. She's the best contradiction I've ever encountered. She glances at me over her shoulder and raises a finger to her lips. Early moonlight streams through the window, lighting up Claire's mischievous expression. I smile at her.

I follow Claire around the corner of the hall and down three steps until we're on a secluded landing, hidden between the entrance to the basement and a closet.

"Is this where you take all your secret lovers?" I whisper to her in the near-dark.

"Only the lucky ones."

I snort, my hands wrapping around her lower back as I tug her against me. Her hands rest on my biceps and she pushes up on her toes, her breasts dragging up my chest.

"Thank you for today with my dad. Really." I hear the sincerity in her tone and it scrapes at my own insecurities.

Sweet Claire has never had anyone go to bat for her, not in the way she needs anyway. I drop my lips closer to hers. "Haven't you realized yet that I'd do anything for you?"

I can just make out her expression in the dim lighting. Tenderness sweeps her gaze as she lifts her mouth to close the several inches that separate us. Then, she's kissing me, I'm responding, and the rest of the world fades away.

The heat of Claire's mouth drags me under, more potent than vodka. Her touch brands my skin, making me hers. I lift her up and her legs automatically encircle my hips. I'm already hard, desperate and ready to be inside of her. With Claire, I go from zero to one hundred in the blink of an eye. I've never had such a visceral reaction to a woman before—well, not since I was a fifteen-year-old inexperienced punk.

"Claire," I murmur, kissing down the column of her neck. "We need to get back." We need to stop this before I take her right here, pinned up against the wall of her parents' closet.

"Shh, not yet," she pants.

My hand slides up under her shirt, feeling her smooth skin. Her breast practically pushes into my palm, as hungry for my touch as I crave the feel of her. She tilts her pelvis upward to rock against me and I swear, pulling my mouth back to hers.

The sound of the door opening takes us both by surprise. It happens so quickly and unexpectedly that we have no time to untangle our limbs. Light streams into our hidden alcove and a very angry Austin shadows the doorframe.

"Fuck," I swear, dropping my head to Claire's shoulder. Slowly I drag my hand out from under her shirt.

She whimpers and I hear Austin's breath hitch in horror.

Gently, I lower Claire to her feet, keeping her frame half behind mine as I turn to meet the fury of my best friend. It's rolling off of him in waves, crashing over Claire and me like a bolt of lightning from Zeus.

Austin points at his sister. "Go." His tone is menacing and dangerously quiet. I recognize the rage in his expression, the betrayal in his eyes, the slipping control he has on his restraint.

Claire inches forward but I grip her wrist and keep her behind me. No way am I letting Claire just walk away like this doesn't concern her. We're together now, even if we didn't announce it to the entire Merrick clan, and I won't have her walking away from me like her place isn't by my side.

Austin's eyes narrow. "What the fuck are you doing?" he growls at me.

"Aus—" Claire starts forward again but I grip her hand tighter. She snaps her mouth shut.

"We need to talk, Austin," I keep my tone level.

"No shit."

"Not here." I shake my head. "Let's go back inside and say good night to your parents. Then, we'll head to my house."

Austin chuckles humorlessly. "Why? You don't want them to know that you're fucking my sister?"

"Watch your mouth," I bite back.

Austin has the sense to look contrite. "I can't believe this."

"It's not what you think," I tell him. Claire's hand

grows rigid in mine. I swipe my thumb across her knuckles to reassure her.

Austin glowers. "What the fuck does that mean, East?"

"It means that I care about Claire. This thing between us is real, Austin. She's not just some girl. She's fucking everything. So we'll go to my place and I'll answer your questions out of respect for our friendship, your relationship with Claire, and your family. But don't get it twisted, we don't owe you anything and you won't be ordering Claire around like she's a little kid. She's all grown up now and capable of making her own decisions. About where she lives, what type of work she does, and who she dates."

Claire sucks in a sharp inhale. My best friend stares at me for three long seconds like he doesn't recognize me. But I don't care. I'm putting Claire first. I'll *always* put her first.

"Let's go." Austin jerks his head to the side.

Claire and I shuffle out of the space, and I got to give my girl credit, she keeps her shoulders back and her head up. We exchange a series of awkward goodbyes with the other Merricks. Mary's brow furrows in concern and Indy shoots Claire a worried glance, but we're out the front door before anyone can start asking questions.

"Get in my car, Claire," Austin demands. I cut him a look and he swears. "Please."

Claire nods and looks at me. I offer her a reassuring nod. The last thing I want is to ruin Claire's relationship with anyone in her family. I slide behind the wheel of my car and make sure Austin is ready before I pull out of the Merricks' driveway and point the car toward my home.

The ride passes slowly and quickly. Time is strange like that. On the one hand, my concern for Claire is heightened, drawing my ire at every red light. I know Austin would never yell at her, but I'm sure he's questioning her pretty hard. Not that Claire can't take it but still, I'd like to be there for her. On the other hand, the extra time seems necessary to ensure that Austin and I both cool down some. The last thing I want is to end up exchanging blows with my best friend.

I park in front of my brownstone and Austin parks a couple car lengths ahead. When he and Claire exit the car, I hold open the front gate and the three of us walk up the steps. Claire punches in the code to unlock the door and I don't miss the furrow of Austin's brow. It's like he's realizing for the first time just how interconnected his sister's and my lives are. Good.

Once we settle inside, Claire wordlessly approaches the Nespresso machine and pops in a capsule. "Let's sit down and talk rationally," she says, sounding much older than her twenty-four years.

Austin stays standing behind a barstool and glares at me. "How did this start?" he demands, his finger wagging between Claire and me. "You guys hated each other."

"There's a thin line between love and hate," Claire points out. She sets down Austin's coffee mug.

Austin snorts, his glare hardening. "Love?" He snaps his neck in my direction. "Is that what you fucking told her? That you love her? Did you seduce my baby sister, Easton?"

"Austin, stop." Claire angles herself in between us even though we're standing on opposite sides of the kitchen island. "Easton didn't *seduce* me; this isn't Victorian England. I don't need you to protect my honor. I've wanted East for years and when I moved in here, I made sure he knew it."

Austin and I both swing our heads toward Claire. She slips onto a barstool, unfazed, and takes a long sip of her coffee. "Do you want a tea, East? I think any caffeine will make it tough to sleep tonight."

I shake my head, in awe of her blasé attitude.

"Okay." She turns back toward her brother. "This is how this is going to go. You"—she points at Austin—"are you going to realize that I am an adult. I am dating Easton Scotch because I want to and for some unfathomable reason, because he sees something in me that everyone else seems to overlook."

Austin flinches but keeps his mouth shut.

"And you"—Claire points at me—"are going to continue to show up for yourself, for your team, and for me. We'll tell the rest of my family that we're dating when we're ready but preferably sooner rather than later."

I nod.

"The two of you are going to sit at this island and talk like men. You are best friends, you are on the same hockey team, and you both love and want to protect this girl right here." She points to herself. "I won't have this tension between you guys. So I'm asking you, for me, to please sort out your shit so we can move forward." She stands from the kitchen island, taking her coffee mug with her. "I'll be downstairs watching *The Real Housewives of New Jersey*. Holler if you need me, but if you don't get it together, I can't promise that I won't flip tables like Teresa."

With that, Claire removes herself from the kitchen.

Austin and I glare at each other. I sigh, deciding to man up. "I care about her, man. A lot."

Austin narrows his gaze. "Why didn't you tell me?"

I raise my hands in the air. "Because I'm a fuckup, Austin. I know it; you know it. But that girl"—I point to the doorway Claire disappeared through—"believes in me. She's been helping me more than you can ever imagine. I'm trying to be enough for *her* and in order to do that, I can't deal with the noise that everyone else is going to throw our way. This thing between us is too new. We're too fragile. And I'm still too fucked up."

Austin scrapes his hand over his face. "How long?"

"Almost two months."

He swears. "You're for real?"

I nod. "I'll be good to your sister, Austin. I'll always put her first. I'll always protect her, even from myself if I have to."

"What's that mean, Easton?" His voice is sharp.

"It means that Claire is my priority. More than worrying about your hurt feelings or how pissed off Joe is going to be. More than my playing hockey or having all of this." I throw my arms out wide. "Some days, I only show up because she believes I will. She's keeping me going, Austin. And I won't take advantage of her heart, even if I have to hurt mine to protect hers."

Austin considers my words for a long minute before nodding. "I'm still pissed as fuck at you."

"I know."

"Treat her right."

"I will."

"We put this behind us on the ice. Put the team first."

"I agree."

He nods, moving toward the door. "But I'm not ready to sit at your table and shoot the shit. Right now, I want to put my fist through your face. You lied to me, Easton."

I shake my head. "I never lied to you, Austin."

"It was a lie by omission."

"My loyalty is to Claire," I tell him, so he knows exactly where I stand.

He considers this, nodding once. "I guess I can't be mad at that because I'd want the guy my sister's dating to put her first." He glares at me. "I just wish it wasn't you."

His words plow into the center of my chest like the punch from a MMA champion. It's a devastating blow and it takes me a moment to find my voice. "I understand."

"Good," Austin says, opening the front door and stepping outside. He doesn't look back.

I close the door after him. A heavy silence settles over the house. I know that Claire and I did the right thing by standing up for ourselves, for what's between us. I know I did the right, mature, manly thing by speaking with Austin one-on-one.

I *know* it. But I don't feel it. My chest tightens and pressure builds in my head until my temples pound.

If I did everything the way I was supposed to, why the hell do I feel so off-balance? Like I just shifted our lives a quarter of an inch in the wrong direction and now, the foundation that connects me, Claire, Austin, Noah, Indy, all the Merricks, is on shaky ground?

CHAPTER 18
CLAIRE

"Hey! How was practice?" I ask Easton when he comes through the front door.

He pauses, his eyes shuttering closed. He brushes a hand through his hair, and stows his practice bag. "Fine."

"You hungry?" I lean my shoulder against the door-frame and study him. Shadows are stamped beneath his eyes and he hasn't shaved since Sunday. He looks exhausted, but it's more than that. Ever since he spoke to Austin, he's been aloof and distant toward me.

"Nah. Already ate." He shuts the closet door and scrubs a hand over his face, his finger tracing his scar.

"Okay," I blow out a breath. "Do you want to —"

"I have some videos I need to watch before Thursday's game." He cuts me off and strides toward the stairs. "It's going to be a late night for me so…don't wait up." He drops his head so he doesn't have to meet my eyes. In the next blink, he's halfway up the staircase.

I stare after him, my mouth dropped open in disbelief. Coldness trickles down my back and my stomach turns. Is Easton blowing me off? Did he have a tough few days at practice? Does he need some space? Even as the thoughts flit through my mind, I recognize them for what they are. Excuses.

Instead of manning up and having a real conversation with me, Easton is pushing me away. He's showing me that he's done with me. That things with my brother, with the team, are too rocky for him to want to fight for us. For me.

His dismissal hurts more than I thought it would. It hurts a hell of a lot more than it used to before we became roommates, before he kissed me like he meant it. I press the heel of my hand into the center of my chest, trying to alleviate some of the pressure gathering there. For the third night in a row, I occupy my time with reality TV, praying that Easton will make an appearance, that he'll invite me back into his bed. Instead, I sleep alone. When I wake in the morning, he's already gone.

His absence feels devastating, shattering my heart and causing my mind to jump into overdrive. I can't focus on anything that isn't related to him and after writing my third shitty cover letter, I blow off my job search and text Rielle. My desperation must come through in the message because she agrees to meet for a coffee even though she's at work.

Forty minutes later, I'm sitting in the back of our favorite coffee spot, about to sob into a plate of scones.

"What happened?" Rielle asks, her gaze sympathetic.

"It's awful," I lament, tucking my hair behind my ears. "Austin caught us—"

"Having sex?" she gasps.

I snort a half laugh, half sob, and shake my head. "No, thank God, no. We were just kissing but he's furious."

"How furious?" Rielle lifts a skeptical eyebrow.

"Angrier than the time we used his air hockey table to play Alcohockey."

Rielle sputters on her macchiato, pressing the back of her hand to her mouth. "Damn, he was pissed that night. In all fairness, we were drunk."

"He was furious that we cut the holes in it for our Solo cups."

She snickers. "I forgot we did that. How the hell did we manage power tools drunk?"

"I have no idea," I say, ripping a scone in half and stuffing my face. Let it be known that Claire Merrick excels at emotional eating. It's one of my many talents.

"What happened after Austin saw you?" She gentles her tone.

"He came back to Easton's place and I tried to lay down the law."

Rielle raises another eyebrow. *Why doesn't anyone take me seriously?*

"By your expression, I'm sure you know it didn't work."

"They fought?" she asks and I don't miss the glimmer of excitement in her eyes.

I roll mine. "No, Rielle. Easton basically told Austin that our relationship was none of his business and to back off."

Rielle's mouth drops open. "Are you kidding me?" she whispers excitedly. "Holy shit, Claire, he really likes you."

I narrow my eyes. "That's what I've been saying. We're in this together."

"Yeah"—she waves a hand—"but I didn't realize that he'd go to bat for you like that. Go against Austin."

"And stick up for me with Dad."

"What?"

I fill her in on Easton having my back with the band logos and album covers.

Rielle nods along, her expression growing more curious with each sentence I share. "Babe." She pushes the plate of scones closer to me so I can start my second one. "I don't get it. This is good, right? You've wanted Easton for so long and here he is, sticking up for you with your family, going all in with you, for you. Why are you crying?"

I close my eyes. The next part is too dreadful to admit aloud. To Rielle's credit, she waits patiently, knowing I'm going to cave and tell her all the worried thoughts clanging around in my head.

I take a steadying breath and admit, "I think he regrets it."

She's quiet and I force my eyes open.

Rielle studies me for a long moment, her expression serious. "You think he regrets sticking up for you or ..."

"I don't know," I admit. "But on Sunday, we were making out like teenagers at my parents' house and for the past couple of days, he's gone by the time I wake up. Last night, he didn't even want us to sleep together. He comes home late at night and mentions something about watching hockey reels or studying plays, and crashes early." I shake my head. "He's freezing me out, Rielle. Last week, I was mentally planning our future, and now I'm waiting for him to end things with me."

Rielle frowns and bites her bottom lip as she considers my words. "Do you think it was too much too soon?"

"What do you mean?"

"Claire, he just got out of rehab a few months ago. In that time, he had to start over with his team, accept that Noah is with Indy now and has his own life, and got pretty serious with you. The only family he has, not counting Noah, is yours. If he feels like his relationship with them is on shaky ground"—she shrugs—"maybe he's just processing it all and everything is too overwhelming?"

"Maybe," I admit, hating that she could be right. Did I somehow push Easton too close to the edge? Is his relationship with me, or the fallout with Austin, going to trigger him to make a decision that ends with him losing his AA gold coin?

Dread weighs heavy in my chest as I consider the possibility of being responsible for Easton's downward spiral. Guilt churns in my stomach and I push the plate of scones away.

"Claire."

I look up into the wise eyes of my best friend. She places a hand on my wrist, leaning forward until the ends of her dark hair drag across the table. She lowers her voice. "This isn't your fault."

"What if it is?" I whisper, both relieved and embarrassed that she can read my thoughts.

"It's not. You've been in love with Easton for—"

"For forever," I finish her sentence. "What if his feelings for me aren't real? I mean, what if he thinks they are because he's so caught up in the moment. But what if I'm really just a distraction for him while the rest of his life seems out of his control? "Oh my God," I whisper as horror washes over me. "Do you think I'm his crutch?"

Rielle bites her bottom lip again. It's something she does when she has a million things to say but doesn't know if she should say them or not.

"Say it," I urge her.

"I don't know." She shakes her head, looking miserable. "At first, I thought *maybe*."

"Why didn't you say anything?"

"Because you were so happy," she admits. "And you

deserve to be happy, Claire. I know this past year has been tough on you with your job search. Savannah's in New York now, Indy is having a baby, and I know that I'm never really around." Her eyes darken and an expression I don't understand ripples across her face. She clears her throat and her face smooths out once more. "Easton filled you up with so much of your bubbly sparkle and it looked really good on you. I didn't want to fill your head with pessimistic shit when you were blissed out. Besides, I didn't really *know*. I've never seen you with East. When you told me how he stood up for you with your family… I do think he has deeper feelings for you. It's just that all of it at once, right now, could be a lot for him."

I nod, thinking over her words. "Yeah, maybe."

"You've got two options."

I glance at Rielle, waiting for her to continue.

"Either press him for an answer or give him some space."

I sigh, leaning back in my seat. "I don't want to put him on the spot. Besides, he's leaving for an away game tonight. He'll be gone 'til Friday."

"Then why don't you suggest that he hang out with Noah, have a guys' night on Friday or Saturday. Maybe his brother can help him come to terms with his strain with Austin, help him sort through his thoughts. And you come out with me."

My mouth drops open. "Go out with you? Ri, I've been begging you for months to go clubbing with me. Or at least drinks that aren't at Indy's or your place."

She sighs, rubbing her fingers over her forehead. "I know. I've been a shit friend, Claire. But things have been so hectic at work and I, well, I need to blow off some steam too."

I narrow my eyes at her cryptic message. "What's going on?"

She shakes her head and gives me a quick smile. "Nothing. We're not talking about me today; we're focusing on you. What do you say? Out this weekend?"

I hesitate, not wanting to shoot Rielle down when I've been trying since summer to get her to party with me. On the other hand, Aiden Hardsin, Indy's best friend, reached out about seeing Big Roxi perform on Saturday night. "Aiden, Indy's friend—"

"The entertainment lawyer?"

"Yeah. He invited me to tag along with him on Saturday. He's going to check out a bluegrass band and later on, a rapper who's performing near you. Do you want to come? We can always hit up a club afterwards." I force myself to tack on the last part. Because now, a night out in a dark club with pulsing energy and reckless decisions isn't as tempting as it was a few months ago. I used to crave nights out, now I crave nights in on the couch with Easton. Thank God Indy encouraged Aiden to reach out to me. Otherwise, I wouldn't be hitting the music scene looking for clients as hard as I should. And my social life would be nonexistent.

Rielle smiles, her expression devoid of judgement. "Sure, that sounds cool." She stands from the table. "I'm sorry, babe. But I really have to get back to work. Let me know about this weekend. If you don't want to party, we can always grab dinner before we meet up with Aiden."

"Yeah, that could work," I agree.

"You want to head out with me or hang for a bit?"

I glance around the quiet coffee shop. There's a lull in activity, the period between lunch and the after-work crowd. If I go back to Easton's, I'll risk disrupting his mood and feeling even worse about myself. I glance at the plate with half a scone left.

"I'll hang for a bit."

"Okay." Rielle wraps her arm around my neck in a quick hug. "I'll talk to you later. Call me if you need me. For real." She fixes me with a look.

I manage a small smile. "Promise."

"You'll be okay, Claire," she says with a wave.

I watch her leave and blow out a sigh. A wave of emotion rumbles through me as I recall the past few nights. The loneliness that stabbed me when Easton would come home and glance at me with barely concealed hurt in his eyes. It's like my presence pains him. Gone are the warm embraces and steamy exchanges. For weeks, we couldn't get enough of each other, our bodies so in sync I wondered how I lived so long and dated, without experiencing the intensity and passion I shared with Easton.

Now, we walk around each other on eggshells. We exist in each other's space without connecting. Everything is polite and cordial, cold and stiff. I look at him and see both a man I love struggling and a stranger I don't recognize.

How can so much change in such a short amount of time? How can I be in the same room as Easton and feel like he's half a world away?

I finish the rest of the second scone as my phone beeps.

Glancing down at the incoming email, my heart lodges in my throat when I read the subject line.

Phone Interview.

My fingers tremble as I swipe to open the email, my eyes scanning the message rapidly. A pharmaceutical company in New Jersey is looking for a graphic designer to join their pharmaceutical packaging team. It's an entry-level position with a standard salary and benefits package. I work a swallow. A tinge of pride rises in my throat but it's stamped out by the realization that I would spend my entire day designing standard, straightforward, generic medical packaging. It's a far cry from the exciting, creative, edgy album covers I've been doing in recent weeks.

Still, it's a job. A real, nine-to-five, I'll-have-fourteen-vacation-days-a-year kind of job that will make my father proud.

I blow out a deep breath and drop my phone into my purse. Even though I should be happy and relieved, my good feelings are overshadowed by Easton's distance. I always thought my friends who got so caught up in guys were silly, but now I realize how hard it is to battle against the emotions of being hopelessly and desperately in love with someone.

It's awful.

Standing from my chair, I grab my wallet and walk to the counter. Then, I order another latte and a chocolate chip cookie.

Austin's glare is pure steel as he skates past me. I turn and stare at him but he keeps skating, calling out to Torsten and James, our defensive line.

Noah's hand settles on my shoulder. "Easy."

I stare at my brother. Everything about him is different than me. Where he's got dark eyes, I've inherited my father's blue. Where he's dependable and responsible, I'm reckless and wild. Noah is a model citizen and I walk the edge. He can manage his liquor and I'm a damn alcoholic.

How can two brothers be so vastly different?

We were raised the same, with bitter, neglectful parents, in a hollow, tense house. We grew up on sharp pinches and cutting remarks. We both poured our energy and focus into hockey.

But Noah's always been the better of the two of us. Most of the hockey introductions I got were because of him. His prowess on the ice led to a better contract for me when he packaged us as a duo. My whole life, my brother has had my back. Everyone knows I wouldn't be the player I am without Noah.

Especially my father.

Staring into the eyes that are opposite of mine, I recall the nights Dad set up the net in the back of the house. It was blistering cold. The kind of cold that freezes parts of your anatomy and makes hot air burn more than soothe. For hours, Dad would slap empty beer bottles and cans at my head. He'd remind me, with his strength and with his words, that I'd be completely worthless, more worthless than him, if it wasn't for Noah.

But I was a cocky motherfucker with an overly healthy sense of self.

It isn't until right now, this moment, that I realize Dad was right. My glove reaches up to trace the scar through my eyebrow, but my visor is in the way and my hand drops.

If it wasn't for Noah, I would have already plunged down the drain, not just circled around it.

A man like my brother is worthy of his fat paycheck, his adoring fans, a woman like Indy. A guy like me only has a paycheck because of him, only has fans because of him, and will never keep a woman like Claire.

"Hey." Noah shakes my shoulder. "What the hell are you thinking about?" He smacks my helmet, peering at me intently. "You good?"

"Yeah." I clear my throat, shaking off his touch. The last thing I deserve is comfort. "Fine."

Noah gives me another searching look. I can tell he's trying to get a read on me. His brow furrows in worry and I fucking hate it. Hate that after all these years, Noah is still saddled with worrying about me.

I also hate that I can't get my head straight after Sunday night. It's messed up. I don't know exactly what changed but now that Austin knows about Claire and me, all of the worries I had about our relationship have risen to the surface. We're no longer wrapped in our honeymoon period but plunged into reality. If Claire and I plan a future the way I want to, will she inherit all of the concern Noah manages on my behalf? Will her days be spent mulling over my shifting moods? Will she hide her worry behind nervous smiles? Will panic seize her thoughts when there's traffic and I'm late coming home? A million scenarios flood my mind and all of them suck. Because all of them show—with disturbing clarity—what an energy drain I am on those closest to me.

"We're lining up." Noah's voice is clipped.

I nod and skate to my position for the face-off. We're scrimmaging today. Tonight, we fly out to Houston. Next week, we have three tough games against fierce competition. The puck drops and Austin gains control, flipping it to Noah even though I'm open. I snort, knowing the game he's playing.

Anger—at Austin, at my father, at myself—fuels me. I let it simmer in my veins, use it to my advantage to get me through the scrimmage. Thanks to my brother, I have years of muscle memory to rely on because today, my heart isn't in it.

"YOU LOOK LIKE SHIT," Torsten says. He holds the door open for me as I leave the arena.

I was hoping to sneak out without anyone noticing but Torsten was three steps ahead of me, in his own rush to leave after today's practice.

"Not sleeping great," I reply, my voice gruff.

His grin falls and he narrows his eyes at me. "You okay?"

"Yep." My lips make a popping sound on the *p* and I know Torsten knows I'm full of shit. I fix the strap of my duffle bag, hitching it higher on my shoulder.

"Come on, dude, whatever's going on with you and Austin is going to blow over."

I shake my head. "Not this time."

Torsten frowns. He crosses his arms over his chest, shifting his position to shield his face from the wind. "Whatever it is can't be that bad. Unless you drank all of Mary's good wine or made a pass at Claire—"

My eyes jerk up to his at the mention of her name.

He reads the situation immediately and swears. "You and Claire?"

I nod.

"You kidding me? Claire Merrick is not just some—"

"Don't finish that sentence," I warn him, stepping closer. "I know exactly who Claire is. I know I'm not good for her. I know I'll never be worthy of her. I know it and I did it anyway because she's fucking...Claire." I sigh, raking a hand across my face. The last thing I want to do is get into it with my team. But it's too late for that now. "It wasn't some random hookup, okay? I care about her, man."

Torsten stares at me for a long moment before nodding. He steps back and shakes his head at me. "Whenever you fuck up, Scotch, you go all fucking in. I swear I've never seen a guy take more risks with his future, with his friendships, than you. One day, you're going to have to own up to the shit you pull. Make this right with Austin. The team is counting on it. And don't fuck around with Claire. She doesn't deserve your bullshit. Make things right with her before you get on the plane tonight."

I bite my lip and turn away even though I really want to cock my fist back and ram it down Torsten's throat. But I don't, because he's right. The last three times I went out with Torsten, I went home with a different girl. One time, we didn't even make it home. I fucked her in the men's bathroom and Torsten walked in on us. Of course he doesn't want me around Claire. She's the team's surrogate little sister and I'm the guy who screws everything up.

The only reason I haven't gotten my ass handed to me yet is because of Austin and Noah.

And now, I've completely lost Austin's trust too.

"Fuck," I swear, throwing my bag in the trunk of my car. I slide behind the wheel and drive home. A part of me hopes that Claire is there so I can wrap her in my arms, kiss her senseless, and feel something other than self-hate and despair.

But the smarter part of me wishes she's already packed her bags and bounced. Because while I'm not strong enough to stay away from Claire the way I should, she's sensible to know better than to hang around for me. The only thing I can offer is heartbreak and the only heart I ever gave a shit about not breaking is Claire's.

When I get home, disappointment fills me. She's not here. The house is spotless, everything perfectly in its place just the way she likes it. But her warmth is missing, casting my home in a dull grey.

I pour a glass of water and plop down on a kitchen barstool. Glancing at my phone, I ignore the messages from Noah checking on me. His concern causes more guilt to layer in my stomach. When is Noah going to learn that he can't single-handedly save me? That most days, I'm not even worth saving?

I gulp the water back in three swallows. The front door opens and I pause, my gaze whipping to the foyer.

My angel steps through the door, her blonde hair piled on her head like a halo. She moves slowly, as if she's in a daze. I frown and sit up straighter as she makes her way toward the kitchen, dropping her bag at the foot of the stairs.

When she enters the kitchen, she jumps, pressing the heel of her hand to her chest. "You scared me."

"Sorry," I say, not sounding sorry at all. What else is new?

"I didn't think you'd be here."

"Practice ended early."

She nods, helping herself to a glass of water. I watch her movements, noting the detachedness between her actions and her thoughts. She seems sluggish. When she looks up, I see that her eyes are rimmed in red, her eyelids puffy.

It hits me like a sucker punch. I made Claire, my Claire, cry. In this moment, I hate myself even more than I did the night Dad's beer bottle smashed into my eyebrow, slicing it wide open and resulting in five stitches. That night, I resented myself for letting him get the best of me. Right now, I resent myself for ever putting Claire in this position.

I took advantage of her goodness, her sweetness, and now, I sliced her open and made her tears rain down. I'm dying to go to her. To wrap her in my arms, tug her against my chest, and breathe in the scent of her hair. I want to whisper reassurances in her ear, press my lips over her skin, and coax her body and mind to relax.

Instead, I force myself to remain seated. My hands fall to my lap, curling into fists under the kitchen island and out of Claire's sight. I don't want her to know how much she affects me. I want her to move on so she can have the life she deserves. With a man who deserves her.

God, the thought of her with another guy cuts deep.

My chest burns like an army of fire ants invaded the space and my foot taps a staccato against the bottom rung of the barstool.

Claire places down her water glass. The silence in the kitchen continues, adding a glare of anger to our silent standoff.

"Are you going to say anything?" she asks me quietly.

"I fly to Houston tonight."

"Yeah."

"I'm back tomorrow night. I'm going to spend a few nights at Panda's," I force out.

Her face falls. "You don't have to do that. I can be out of here by the time you get back tomorrow."

No! I want to shout it loud enough to burst the fucking windows. Instead I shake my head. "Stay. This is your place too."

She scoffs.

I pinch the bridge of my nose, praying for some mental clarity. "I just need a minute, Claire. I need some time, some space, to work through all the shit in my head."

"You could talk to me," she offers.

I shake my head. "It's not pretty, babe."

"I don't care." The second she says it, I know she means it, and that makes me feel worse.

"I know you don't," I admit, feeling more for her in this moment than I ever have. The emotions rush over me, drowning me in their intensity. For a second, all I can do is stare at her sapphire eyes, the freckle that dots just below the right corner of her mouth and wish that things between us could be different. That *I* could be different. Less like me.

"I don't want you to move out. I know I haven't been fair to you. I've been shutting you out since Sunday and Austin...I just, I need a minute," I repeat.

She nods, tears filling her eyes. To her credit, she doesn't let them fall. "Okay."

I slip off the barstool. "I gotta pack. I'll check back in with you sometime Saturday."

"Sure," she agrees noncommittally.

When I get to the stairs, I force myself to turn away. I pack my bag, take a quick shower, and get ready to head to the airport. By the time I come back downstairs, Claire is gone.

CHAPTER 20
CLAIRE

Because I'm a masochist, I watch Easton's game in Houston. For the first time this season, he edges Sims out for playing time and spends the entire third period on the ice. Watching him weave effortlessly through players, maneuvering the puck like it's an extension of his stick, leaves me a little breathless. He's focused and intense, a quiet strength and skill humming around him like an aura.

I sit perched on the edge of the couch in East's game room, my fingernails in my mouth, as I watch Easton the hockey god rise from the ashes like a phoenix. His play is breathtaking, reminiscent of his past seasons, before he spiraled, before he ended up making waves because of his alcoholism.

Tonight's Easton is the man I first fell in love with and I cling to the images of him on ESPN with my breath frozen in my throat and my eyes tearing. After Easton's final goal, the Hawks win 6–3. Easton had two goals and an assist, making him a celebrated hero in a matter of hours.

I turn the television off as soon as the game ends. Tonight, the team will party hard. Easton will be pulled into the excitement of a huge win, feeling his own personal accomplishments, and walk into any club like he owns it.

All the thoughts of what can go wrong clang in my head and I squeeze my eyes closed tight. I hate that I'm so caught up on him. I hate that I've made my world revolve around him and his feelings toward me. For years, I've watched Easton from afar. I had big feelings for him but I knew how to navigate them. Thinking he'd never be attracted to me, I still went out, partied, dated, had fun. But now, knowing that Easton is slipping further away with each passing day, I can't bring myself to do anything but mope.

"Aagh," I let out a strangled, pissed-off cry and flop back on the couch. I need to get my life together. I can't just exist in this emotional limbo while Easton takes time for himself.

I need to take time for myself too.

Forcing myself to sit up, I grab my phone. I ignore the stab of disappointment that there's no message from East. Not even one asking me if I watched the game.

I open my email app and double-check the time of my phone interview for tomorrow. 11a.m. Although I'm not particularly excited about designing medical packaging, even I know better than to pass up on an interview opportunity.

Easton was always a long shot. The old adage—if it seems too good to be true, it usually is—comes to mind.

Sighing, I get to my feet, make my way upstairs, take a shower, and throw myself into bed. Tomorrow, I'm turning over a new leaf. Tomorrow, I'm going to secure a job offer for myself.

Tomorrow, my heart will ache a little less.

"TELL ME EVERYTHING," Indy demands, pushing past me in the foyer and making her way to the kitchen. She helps herself immediately to a decaf Nespresso pod. "I'm too cheap to buy one of these," she tells me over her shoulder, "but I'm a little bit obsessed."

I roll my eyes and settle back on my barstool. "Want some waffles?" I pour a healthy serving of syrup over mine.

"No, thanks. I ate already." Indy leans back against the counter as she waits for her coffee. "I can't believe you didn't tell me about the phone interview. I could have helped you prep."

"You're the *only* person I've told. And I didn't need help prepping. But thank you," I add when I see her expression.

"Wait, you haven't told your parents yet?"

I shake my head.

"Austin?"

"Nope."

"East?"

I glare at her.

"Why haven't you told anyone?" she asks, incredulous.

I chew a big bite of my delicious Belgian waffle with extra maple goodness. It's just like the Scotch brothers to own something like a fancy waffle maker that's never been used. Until now.

"Well, for starters, I want to see if I get it first."

"Fair."

"And," I add, knowing I'll only admit the truth to her and Rielle, "I'm not sure if I even want it."

Indy makes a face. "Why not? It's a solid entry-level position with a reputable company."

"In New Jersey," I point out.

Indy shrugs. "Sometimes you have to move to the opportunity."

"Doing medical packaging."

"It's a graphic design position."

I scrunch up my nose as Indy watches me thoughtfully.

"Your heart's not in it," she states.

"My heart's not in it," I agree.

"Are you still going to hear that rapper with Aiden on Saturday?"

I nod.

"Any word from East?"

I shake my head, pressing my lips together to hold back the emotion that swells up at the mention of his name.

Indy gives me an empathetic look. "I'm sorry, Claire. I hate that he's making you feel like this."

"But?" I prod, knowing there's more she wants to say.

"But don't you feel like things happened really fast between y'all? I mean, in a matter of weeks, you went from glaring at each other and having your feelings hurt because he called you 'kid' to getting naked with him and planning a future."

I sigh, hating that Indy is echoing Rielle. Still, I can't just dismiss her observation since it's now the second time I've heard it. "Maybe."

"He needs time," she says. "And you can't just wait around for him while he takes it."

"I hate feeling like I'm in limbo," I admit. "I don't know where I stand with him and it's driving me nuts. The waiting is almost worse than the knowing, even if his decision isn't the one I want."

"Well what about what *you* want?" Indy asks, taking a sip of her coffee. "You don't have to wait around for him. You're choosing to."

I let those words sink in and nod slowly. "You're right."

"Take time for yourself too, Claire. Think about the type of future you want. Easton is a great guy. He's Noah's brother and my baby's uncle and I care about him. But I care about you too. East's recovery is new. And fragile. You will always worry about him. There may be more periods where he needs time and space. Are you okay with that? Can you live like this?" she asks, gesturing at me.

I bite the corner of my lip. *Can I live like this?* My stomach is in knots and my throat is closing with too many desperate feelings that have nowhere to go. I feel useless and worthless and…hurt. "I don't know," I admit.

Indy lifts an eyebrow but her tone is gentle when she says, "Well, now is a good time to think about it."

"Yeah," I say. "Rielle asked me to go out Saturday night. After the thing with Aiden. Have a girls' night."

"You haven't had one in a long time."

"I know. I guess I felt…" I trail off, pressing my lips together.

"Guilty," Indy supplies, correctly reading my thoughts. "Because you didn't want to go out and have drinks with Easton sitting at home, working on his sobriety."

"Yes."

"Well, the guys flew home this morning. Noah is sleeping but he told me that Easton decided to crash at Panda's. If he's not back by Saturday…" she lets her sentence linger.

"Then, I'll go out with Rielle. Have a night out to clear my head and have some fun. And pack my bags Sunday morning."

Indy nods, her expression serious. "I think that sounds like a good idea."

I blow out a deep sigh. "Me too." Logically, I think it makes the most sense. But emotionally, the thought of moving out hurts. It hurts deeply and anguish rolls through me.

Not just because I don't want to move back to Mom and Dad's. But because I truly don't want to leave Easton.

CLAIRE

I'm in. Let's go out tonight and do it big.

RIELLE

Thank God! I need to blow off some serious steam.

CLAIRE

???

RIELLE

Not even worth explaining. Just know, I may need to be carried home.

CLAIRE

[thumbs up emoji] I'm on it. I'm meeting Aiden at 9.

RIELLE

Any word from Easton?

CLAIRE

Nada.

RIELLE

Ouch. I'm sorry, babe.

CLAIRE

Maybe for the best?

RIELLE

[shrugging emoji] Promise you'll have fun tonight.

CLAIRE

That's all I can hope for.

RIELLE

I'll come to you. We'll grab an Uber to meet Aiden?

CLAIRE

Good plan. Come at 7 p.m.? Dinner first?

RIELLE

Love it! See you then.

I TOSS my phone on the bed and rummage through my closet. I flip through hangers until I find a killer dress, one I haven't worn in ages. I grin, pulling out the tight, short, sexy navy dress that dips down to just above my navel and makes my eyes pop. It's borderline slutty but in a way that gives me just the extra confidence I need. Especially tonight. I take my time curling the ends of my hair and applying a smokey eye. I color my lips, don massive hoop earrings, and spritz on perfume.

I'm carrying my heels downstairs when the doorbell rings and I pull it wide open for Rielle.

"Damn girl! You look hot!" My best friend's mouth drops open.

I laugh, pulling her into the house and wrapping her in a quick hug. "Let me see what you're wearing."

She shimmies out of her winter coat and I applaud her tiny, black leather miniskirt and sheer white blouse with a cut-out on the sides. "Wow."

"I feel like we're back in college." Rielle laughs, pulling a bottle of vodka from her purse.

I close my eyes and drop my head back. "Rielle, that was just last year."

She laughs louder and pushes past me toward the kitchen.

"Rielle, wait," I say, uneasy about drinking alcohol in Easton's house.

She's rummaging through the cabinets. When she finds the glasses, she grabs two. She glances at me over her shoulder. When she meets my eyes, she freezes. "Shit! I didn't even think." She shakes her head. "I'm sorry, Claire. Let's get out of here. We'll grab drinks at the restaurant."

Relief unspools in my chest. "Okay."

"Can I just use the bathroom first?"

"Of course. Upstairs, first door on the right."

"Thanks." Rielle flashes me a smile and bounds up the stairs.

I finish getting ready, slipping on my shoes and packing my clutch. As soon as Rielle is ready to go, we step outside into the cold night air and take an Uber to a trendy downtown restaurant neither of us have tried before.

By the time Rielle and I meet up with Aiden, I'm already feeling the liquor. I'm a little lightheaded, a lot giggly, and an excellent conversationalist. Aiden Hardsin is easy on the eyes with his messily styled blond hair and big blue eyes. He's dressed like a badass lawyer and a Brooklyn hipster collided—tailored blazer, swanky pocket square, rolled-up jeans with Chelsea boots—and while the look shouldn't work, he pulls it off effortlessly.

"Hey Claire." He hugs me hello, chuckling as I stumble. His hand rests against my back to steady me. "I see you pre-gamed."

I glance back to see if he's pissed since technically, he's here for work. And so am I. But Aiden grins at me, amused, and turns to introduce himself to Rielle.

"Okay," he says as he leads us toward the front of the venue. A line already snakes to the corner of the street and a burly bouncer guards the door with a no-nonsense expression. "We'll grab a few drinks and listen to some of the opening acts. I'd like to connect with Big Roxi before his set since, if all goes well, it will be too hectic afterwards. Make sure you introduce yourself and tell him about your work. Pitch any ideas you have for merchandising too. Do you have a business card?"

I shake my head, sobering. I should have put more thought into this. Why didn't I? Why don't I ever prepare the way I'm supposed to? A flush works up my chest as worry unfurls in my stomach.

Aiden must see my concern because he shakes his head. "I swear, it's super casual. Don't worry about it. I just want to make sure you have your chance to talk to him. Be yourself, Claire. You've got this." Aiden pushes me forward and exchanges a few words with the bouncer.

In the next moment, Rielle and I are walking through a jam-packed venue. It's dark and hazy, and as Rielle grips my hand and turns to look at me over her shoulder, I see the excitement blazing in her eyes.

Aiden guides us toward the bar and asks what we're drinking. After we each take a shot of Fireball, I start to relax. This scene, the club, the pulsing beat, the dreamy expression of music lovers, is one I know well. I can do this.

Aiden, Rielle, and I listen to two opening acts before

we're ushered backstage to chat with Big Roxi. The second I meet him, I'm dazzled. He's got a quiet energy that wraps around him like an aura. His dark eyes are warm, his smile easygoing.

"Hey man, it's good to meet you. I'm Aiden Hardsin with Pierce Parke Entertainment Law Group." Aiden introduces himself. During their exchange, Big Roxi listens attentively and asks a few questions.

All too soon, Aiden places his hand in the center of my back and pushes me forward. "This is Claire Merrick. She's been doing some freelance work for Boston artists, most notably The Burnt Clovers."

Big Roxi looks me over lazily. He crosses his arms over his chest and leans back. "You Derek's girl?"

I chuckle, shaking my head. "Nope, we're just friends." I stick out my hand, which he takes. He studies me while he holds my hand for a beat too long. Satisfied, he drops my hand and nods, smiling warmly.

"Okay then. Well, I've seen some of your work and I'm impressed. I'm looking for some fresh ideas for merchandising. I'm about to go on"—he tips his head toward the stage—"but if you're free to connect, I'd love to talk through some ideas."

"Absolutely. That would be awesome." I slip him a bar napkin with my number and email address on it. "I haven't made business cards or anything yet." I blush.

He chuckles and shakes his head. "I hear you. When things happen in this industry, they're usually unexpected." He slips the bar napkin into his back pocket. "But at the very least, your method is memorable."

I grin, relieved he's receptive to meeting with me even though I'm probably the most underprepared person on the planet.

"I'll hit you up," he says, his voice deep and rumbly.

A woman slips to his side, all beauty and elegance, and squeezes his hand. "Good luck, baby."

He kisses her sweetly and it's obvious that they're together. He turns and glances at Aiden, Rielle, and me. "Catch you guys later?"

We nod and watch as Big Roxi takes the stage. A hum travels through the crowd and the energy shifts. A beat drops and in a matter of seconds, the quiet energy of Big Roxi erupts into a wild torrent of words that are so much deeper than face value.

He unapologetically dives into political issues, economic inequalities, and social injustices with a ferocity that sends shivers up my arms.

"Wow," Rielle breathes next to me.

I nod. "He's incredible."

The woman who kissed him turns toward us and smiles. "This is just the beginning."

I agree, watching Big Roxi's mesmerizing performance. I don't want to miss a second of his set. Aiden shifts us back to the crowd and I soak up the energy of the group. It pulses in my temples and beats through my body. I'm swept away by the moment, reveling in it. When I look up, I catch Aiden's eye and he grins at me. It's like he realizes at the same time I do that I need to be part of this industry, that my soul demands it.

After an hour, we decide to hit Firefly, another downtown club. Aiden tries to beg off but Rielle ropes him into coming along, explaining that we may require a chaperone to see us safely home. At that guilt trip, Aiden has no choice. When we arrive at Firefly, Aiden tips his head toward the bar. We all take a shot and Rielle grabs our hands, trying to pull us toward the dance floor. This time, Aiden is successful in his attempt to stay behind, but I follow Rielle through the swaying bodies until we're in the center of the floor. We raise our arms overhead and our hips swirl to the beat.

I shake my ass, closing my eyes. My head tips back and I feel the ends of my hair tickle my lower back. For the first time in months, the thoughts swirling in my mind fade. My head clears, blissfully numb, and tonight takes over. I revel in the relaxation that flows through my body. I hold on to the giddy feeling in my stomach. I enjoy the music and the dark and the laughter of my best friend.

"I've missed this!" I open my eyes and shout at Rielle.

She smirks. "I've missed you!"

"We need to do this more often!"

She nods vigorously before pulling me back to the bar.

We each take another shot, ignoring the men who circle around us, looking for a way to engage us in conversation. Aiden steps up. "You guys need a bodyguard more than a chaperone," he tells us.

Rielle and I laugh and look at each other. We're both sporting goofy grins. Tonight, it's just me and my best friend again. And I needed it so much more than I realized.

CHAPTER 21

EASTON

"Stop being a pussy," I scold myself. It's freezing outside, with a blustery wind kicking up, and I'm standing on the front porch of my own home, too scared to go inside.

Is she home? Has she packed up and left?

I shuffle my feet on the stoop and rub my hands together, blowing on them to keep warm. I need to man up and go inside.

Forcing myself to punch in the code, I swing open the front door and enter. The kitchen lights are on, which causes relief to flicker in my chest. But the house is eerily quiet and my disappointment flares.

"Claire?" I call out, shaking off my coat and hanging it in the closet. "You home?"

I walk deeper into the house, listening for any sign of her. There's none.

"Shit." I make my way to the kitchen, stopping dead in my tracks when I note the vodka bottle on the kitchen counter. "What the fuck?"

I glare at the bottle, my throat tightening and aching at

the sight of it. So within reach and yet, a fucking ocean away. It's sealed. Thank God, it's sealed. It's a tiny bit less tempting that way. I'd have to break the seal. I wouldn't be able to hide it. I—

I need to stop thinking about the vodka. The way it tastes when it hits the back of my throat, the burn it blazes, and the warmth it spreads through my limbs.

"No. Stop." I clutch the sides of my head, walking a far circle around the bottle. I can't think about it. I can't not think about it either.

God, what a fucking mess I've made. Of course Claire didn't think I'd show up today. Why would she when I've been silent for the past few days? But why would she bring alcohol into my place?

A surge of anger swells in my chest. My fingers tremble, in nerves, in frustration, in *need*.

I slip onto a barstool at the kitchen island and glare at the bottle.

Where is Claire anyway? One look around the kitchen lets me know she's still living here. So, there's that.

My phone beeps and I clutch it like a godsend.

TORSTEN

Claire's at Firefly with her girl. They're lit.

I clutch the phone tightly in my hand, thoughts of Claire, drunk, being swarmed by men who aren't me, makes me see red. Damn it. Of course she's out, having fun with her friend. Why shouldn't she be? She's a gorgeous, engaging woman who doesn't have an alcohol problem.

I frown, realizing just how seldom Claire has gone out since she moved in here. Has she been out at all? Has she been changing her entire social life to accommodate my shortcomings?

And how didn't I realize it sooner?

Guilt and frustration churn in my stomach as I sit at the kitchen island. My gaze lands on the vodka bottle again. I can practically taste it. I want it. I fucking need it. My entire being vibrates with the craving that is wracking through my body like waves on the beach. Never ending and relentless.

My fingers tremble against my lap.

I jump up from the chair and begin pacing.

I just need to distract myself. I could play Xbox. Or watch a movie. Read a book.

That thought makes me laugh, lending some much-needed levity to the moment. I walk to the foyer and pull open the closet door. I should just leave. Go somewhere.

Images of my favorite pubs and bars flare to life in my mind and I squeeze my eyes closed in a shitty attempt to block them out. No, there's nowhere else to go. Only Panda's house, which I left an hour earlier. If I go back there, I'll raise his suspicions for sure.

Or my brother's. But he's spending time with Indy, probably taking photos of her baby bump and gushing over how much her belly has grown in the past week.

My phone beeps again.

TORSTEN

> Claire's on her way home. She's emotional
> and tipsy and some guy Aiden is with her.
> Her friend is still here. I can come to your
> place if you need to go. I just don't want
> to leave Rielle on her own.

Aiden? Who the hell is Aiden? Why do I know that name?

Noah and Indy. Oh yeah, it all comes flooding back. Aiden is Indy's best friend who my brother stupidly tried to set Indy up with. Is he into Claire? Do they know each other? Is he looking out for her or is he just trying to get in her pants? The thought causes a blinding anger to grip me and I resume my pacing. I can't leave now, not when I know she's going to stumble through the front door, drunk and sad and *with another man*. Why the hell would Rielle stay behind and send Claire home with Aiden?

I step back into the kitchen.

My nerves are zinging around my body so quickly, I can't process it all. Anxiety builds in my chest, making it hard to breathe. The vodka calls to me, a silent answer to all the questions in my mind. I hesitate.

Then, I'm striding toward the bottle. I grip it around its neck and hold on tight. My mouth waters and my throat burns. My knuckles turn white and my breathing grows ragged.

No, this isn't the way to handle this.

You know this. You're better than this.

But are you?

You're really just a washed-up hockey player with no talent. The only reason you have a career is because of Noah. The only reason you have a family is because of Austin. The only reason you've made it this long is because of Claire.

Claire.

Don't do this to her, man. If you fall off the wagon tonight, she'll blame herself. Is that what you want? After you already ruined her social life and made her spend the past few months worrying about your unreliable ass?

I slam the bottle down in the center of the island and resume my pacing.

Everything my eyes catch on in the kitchen seems to mock me. My head buzzes and my vision blurs.

Your brother is ten times better than you. Dad's voice rings in my head, hard and cruel.

I rub the scar through my eyebrow, remembering how the blood seeped through my fingers, hot and bright.

Get your shit together, man. Austin snapped at me the second time I turned up to practice drunk, smelling like a distillery and looking like I hadn't slept in days. Had I?

Prove it. Claire challenged me. Show her that I'm worthy, show her that I want her, show her that I can be enough.

But God, that's impossible, isn't it?

I swear, sliding back onto the barstool. I stare at the bottle, the fucking enemy that provides sweet salvation and utter ruination. What if I break the seal just to smell it? Just one deep inhale to clear my head.

No, no, I can't.

But would one small sip really hurt? I've been so goddamn good for so long.

I force my shoulders to press into the backrest of the chair. I can't do it. I can't.

Fuck, why is this so hard? Why am I in agony?

The front door bangs open and a snort followed by a snicker floats into the kitchen.

She's here. Claire's here. I listen for a male voice but none comes.

Relief so overwhelming it makes me want to weep rolls through me.

My body relaxes the tiniest bit. But I can't look away. I can't take my gaze from the bottle. I can't move.

Her footsteps grow closer. They're unsteady and uneven.

What will she think when she sees me? Will she hate me for my weakness? I do.

Will she pack her bag and leave? Who in their right mind would stay?

"What the hell?" Her voice cuts through the air, sharp and severe.

Slowly, I pull my gaze away from the bottle to meet her shocked expression. Fear flares in her irises. She holds her hands up and approaches me slowly, like she would an injured animal. The toe of her heel catches on the grout in the tile and she stumbles a bit but manages to catch herself on the edge of the island.

"What is this?" She grips the neck of the vodka bottle and yanks it away.

I let out a slow breath, my gaze still locked on where Claire holds the bottle.

She narrows her eyes at me before turning around. Quickly, she hurries to the bathroom. I lurch forward in my seat, my hands wrapping around the armrests of the barstool until my fingers ache.

Moments later I hear the toilet flush and anger and relief mix and swell in my chest.

She flushed it. Thank God she flushed it.

Claire reenters the kitchen, looking a bit more sober than she did five minutes ago. She's barefoot now, and so damn beautiful, I want to wrap her in my arms and thank her for saving me again.

"What are you doing?" Her voice is hoarse, brimming with emotion.

"Thank you," I whisper.

Her expression softens, tenderness sweeping her eyes. "Why?"

"It was here when I got home."

She closes her eyes but I don't miss the pain that blooms in them. "Oh, God. I'm so sorry, East." Her eyes pop open again. "I am so fucking sorry."

I shake my head. "Don't be. I needed to be tested."

"You didn't drink it. The seal was still intact."

"I didn't drink it."

"But you wanted to."

"More than you'll ever understand," I admit.

She lets out a shaky breath and strides toward me. In the next instant, I'm in her arms and she's brushing her fingers through my hair. The sounds she makes are nonsensical but reassuring and I hold on to them. Is this what comfort is? Is this what forgiveness feels like?

I close my eyes and rest my head on her shoulder, letting my weakness mix with her strength. I don't deserve this. Don't deserve her.

She tugs me from the barstool and I sink in her arms to the floor of my kitchen. Vulnerability flares to life, making my limbs lock down and my head spin. A million barbs rest on my tongue, ready to shatter Claire's peace offering, to push her away.

I force myself to swallow them back when she says, "I got you, East. I'm here, baby."

My eyes drag closed, heavy. So fucking heavy from so many burdens for so damn long. I clutch at Claire's skin, holding her close and erasing all the space between us. My fingers wrap in her long hair, knotting the strands around my knuckles. I breathe her in, let her sweet floral scent center me.

I have no idea how long we sit in a heap on the kitchen floor. The room grows cold, my anger dies, and exhaustion rolls through me. She guides my face up, forcing my bleary eyes to meet her compassionate ones.

She offers me the smallest of smiles, the greatest of understanding, and presses her lips to mine.

It's my undoing.

CHAPTER 22
CLAIRE

The torture in Easton's eyes breaks my heart. The vulnerability he lets me see is humbling, sobering me faster than a week of sleep and a gallon of coffee. In this moment, I'm right where I want to be, in his arms.

Nothing has changed. We haven't discussed any of the hurt that led to his leaving. We haven't acknowledged the massive elephant that should be sucking all the oxygen from the room. We have hashed out nothing, agreed to nothing, have absolutely nothing concrete between us. And yet, I'm exactly where I want to be.

The moment my lips touch Easton's, I'm home. I don't know if I'm holding him or if he's clinging to me. It doesn't matter. Nothing matters except we're together and it feels right.

The cold tiles bite into my bare knees but I ignore them. My hips ache from holding the same position for so long but it doesn't matter. Easton's skin is hot beneath my touch. His scent soothes the racing of my heart. His mouth on mine is perfection.

I dip my tongue into Easton's mouth and he meets

mine eagerly, our slow, hesitant touches morphing into a need tinged with desperation. His hands move to my hips and he tugs until his frame is looming over mine, covering me. He kisses me deeply, with so much intensity and passion, that I'm dragged under his spell.

His eyes are filled with longing, edged in wild, and colored with gratitude.

"I need you, Claire." His voice is ragged, husky with want, laced with hurt.

"I'm yours," I tell him, my fingers brushing back his hair. "I've always been yours."

At the catch in my voice, something in him breaks. I see the emotion as it blooms in his expression, beautiful and fleeting, like the bang of a firework. His breathing is unsteady as he dips his head again. He kisses me slowly. Soulfully.

His hands explore my body with a heaviness that wasn't there a week ago. It's different now. Thorough and fierce. His touch brands me, a subtle reminder that no man will ever know my body as intimately as he does.

His mouth travels across my cheek, nips on my earlobe, and makes a slow descent down my neck. I arch into him, my hips searching for his. The pressure building inside of me is throbbing and needy. I want him to simultaneously devour and savor me.

His fingers brush against the undersides of my breasts, caressing and teasing.

My hands track his back, pulling his shirt clear off his head so I can press my fingertips into his skin. He unzips my dress and I shimmy out of it. Easton's eyes drink me in like he's never seen a topless woman before and his lips part. I work a swallow, feeling more exposed than I ever have and yet, surer than I've ever been.

Easton's eyes hold mine as he reaches forward and

gently runs the pad of his thumb over my nipple. I inhale sharply as his other fingers brush against me. "You're beautiful, Claire. You're everything, baby. My angel." His voice is low, soothing in its cadence, tense in his need for me to understand.

"I'm in love with you, Easton." I blurt out the words, needing him to know just how deep my feelings are, how much I care. More than I ever thought I was capable of and yet, not enough.

His brows furrow together and pain blooms in his expression. "Why?" he whispers and the disbelief in his tone guts me.

I reach up and place my hand over his, pressing his palm flat over my heart. "Because it's always been you."

His eyes swim with moisture and surprise rocks through me. I've never seen Easton so unguarded before. I've never witnessed him like this, vulnerable and open. I fall a little deeper.

He wets his bottom lip and tips forward, brushing a soft kiss against my mouth. "Let me make love to you, Claire."

"Yes," I agree, my eyes fluttering closed as his weight settles over me.

But in the next instant, I'm being lifted. Easton cradles me in his arms like I'm his most prized possession. He takes the stairs slowly and leads us into his bedroom. He deposits me in the center of his bed like I may shatter. It's a far cry from how he usually tosses me but everything about tonight is different. More.

It's like we're both shedding the layers we wrap ourselves in to shield us from the world. We're peeling them back and exposing ourselves to the only other person who understands. To each other.

Easton sheds his pants and boxers. My tongue darts

over my bottom lip as my gaze falls to his cock. He's so hard for me and knowing that he feels that way about me causes a rush of heat to flood between my legs. He shakes his head, the smallest smirk glancing off his lips.

"Not yet, baby. I promise we'll get there. But tonight, I want to worship you." He moves over me, settling between my thighs. He kisses the side of my neck. "You saved me, Claire." His mouth finds mine, his hands track up my body, and my eyes drop closed.

I reach for him but Easton's hand covers mine, surprising me. "Let's not rush this," he murmurs, his gaze sweeping over my body like a caress.

While I anticipated our coming together for the first time in a week to be frantic and needy, he slows the pace and takes his time, savoring each moment.

One of his hands holds on to my wrists while the other slides down my arm, hooking around my neck. He pulls back and peers into my eyes.

"I'm sorry for everything, Claire."

"Me too, East."

"Let me love you, baby," he murmurs, trailing kisses down my neck before claiming my mouth again.

My thighs clench at the promise behind his words. His fingers knead the back of my neck and I melt into him.

Easton kisses me passionately as his hand roams down the side of my body, wrapping around me. He holds me close, erasing any space between us.

"You're so fucking beautiful, Claire," East whispers in my ear before moving down my body. He pulls my breast into his mouth and I arch into him, my fingers threading through his hair.

I want everything Easton is willing to give. And then some.

At the moan that falls from my lips, Easton switches

gears. He shadows my body with his and pushes inside of me with a slowness that is agonizing. His eyes bore into mine and all of the feelings swirling in them soothe any of my lingering doubts. Easton fills me up and for the first time in a week, I feel like I can breathe again. Our bodies find a rhythm that is ancient yet completely new to me.

"You're so wet for me, Claire," Easton groans.

I close my eyes as pressure builds low in my belly. Easton's lips streak, featherlight, across my cheek, nipping at my ear. My hands clench his back, pulling him deeper into me, as my hips pivot up to meet his.

"So fucking perfect," he murmurs, trailing kisses up my throat until his mouth captures mine.

I don't know how long we spend kissing and touching. Feeling and exploring. Giving and exchanging. I just know that when we break apart, we're lost in each other's eyes and my heart feels ready to burst. When I come down from the blissful high Easton created, my entire life looks different. The world is different.

With Easton's chest pressed against my back and his arms holding me tight, I feel whole. For the first time, I feel like I'm enough. For me. For him. For my future.

I snuggle deeper in his embrace. My body is spent and sated. Easton made me feel so many things at once that I stopped thinking and just lost myself to the moment. The most beautiful moment of my existence.

My eyelids are heavy with sleep and I relax, my body sagging and my mind quieting. Just before sleep takes me, I feel Easton's breath on the shell of my ear.

"I love you, Claire."

I fall asleep with a smile on my lips.

WHEN I WAKE in the morning, pale gray light wraps around the room. My head throbs and I'm unsure if it's from the shots I did with Rielle, the emotional overload of what happened with Easton, or a combination of both. Other than a dull headache, I don't feel too hungover. I turn slowly, smiling when I see the smirk on Easton's face.

"Good morning, Clairebear. How do you feel?"

"Not as bad as I thought."

He frowns but then snorts. "How much did you drink?"

"Rielle has a thing for shots."

"So does Torsten. He said he saw you last night?" Easton pulls me closer to his chest.

I nod, pressing my hands against his hard pecs. "He backed Aiden up in cutting us off," I admit, laughing. "Big Daddy was not happy that I was nearly sobbing at the bar."

Easton's frown is back, his eyes flashing. "Why were you sobbing?"

I lift an eyebrow and apply more pressure to his chest. "Isn't it obvious?"

He sighs. "I'm sorry, baby. I have a lot of apologizing to do."

I shake my head. "I'm glad I came home when I did..."

He catches my meaning and nods, his eyes darkening. "Me too. I need to hit up a meeting today. Talk to Rick. All of this"—he presses his hand flat against the center of my back—"it's a lot of emotions. Highs and lows. I'm not good at navigating them. I usually handled them by drinking my face off."

"We need to do better, East."

"I know. I need to do better."

"You can talk to me, you know?" I say softly, not wanting to push anything but also desperately wanting him to confide in me about real things. His childhood. His past. His triggers. All of it.

He's quiet for a long moment and I hold my breath.

"Noah and I didn't have the best childhood," he says softly.

I glance up at him but keep very still otherwise.

His fingers toy with the ends of my hair. "My mom was too much under my dad's influence, too scared to step up to him. Every year she wilted a little more, let her light die under his darkness, until there wasn't much left. I don't blame her as much. She's weak. But my father"—he pauses, glancing at the ceiling—"my father is a cruel, twisted son of a bitch."

I draw in a breath. I've never heard Easton speak about anyone with such venom in his tone.

"He used to make me stand in the backyard, after everyone else went to bed. He'd put me in the net, even when it was below freezing outside, and shoot beer bottles at my head with a hockey stick." He rubs absently at his forehead and I don't miss the way his thumb rolls over the scar he has there.

My stomach knots, making me feel nauseous. Did his father give him that scar? Was Easton hit as a child? I don't say anything for fear that he'll stop talking.

"My entire life, I've been compared to Noah. Not by Noah, of course. My brother is the only good person I knew until I met yours." He offers me a half smile. "The first time I had dinner at your parents' house, I was petrified I'd do something wrong and we would never be invited back. Your mom was like one of the moms I'd see on TV. I thought it was fake, you know? But then I met your family and God, Claire, I wanted to be part of something like that so badly. And then you guys gave me a chance." He pauses and I inch closer to him, somehow knowing he needs my support for whatever is coming next.

"I screwed up, Claire. I have ruined so many good things and I am tired of being a failure."

"You're not a failure."

He shakes his head, tugging on my hair so I meet his gaze. "Why do you always stick up for me? I have pushed you and your family away countless times. I've made my brother feel guilty anytime he starts to move on with his life because he doesn't want to leave me behind. He shouldn't have to carry that around. I have pushed away everyone who has helped me, who cares about me, including you."

"You're not a failure," I repeat. "You're in recovery. You're learning and growing and evolving. You're doing your best and I'm proud of you."

He shakes his head, his eyes sad. "I don't deserve you, Claire."

"You already have me, East."

"Promise you won't go?" he murmurs, his tone fragile. Child-like.

He breaks my heart and fills my soul at the same time. I press a kiss to the base of his throat. "I promise, Easton. We're in this together. You don't realize how much your support has helped me grow too. You don't see how much good you create in my life. This isn't one-sided. We're a team."

"I won't ever let you give up on your dreams, Claire."

"I know that."

"For this to work, we have to be honest with each

other, upfront about things. It's too easy for me to keep everything locked down and push people, you, away. It's my default. But I swear, I will walk away before I ever hurt you." His voice drops lower, fear flaring in his eyes. "I am not my father."

My chest squeezes painfully. I reach up and place my palm on his cheek. He lowers his face to press a kiss against my lips. "No, you're not. You're mine."

CHAPTER 23
EASTON

I'm rattled. Some may call it circling the drain but after so many close calls, I'm not there yet. Almost but not yet.

I breathe in the cold air of the arena and let it wash over me. Closing my eyes, I focus on the sounds of the space, more familiar to me than anywhere else in the world. The sharp cut of skates on the ice. The near silence of 5 a.m., only permeated by a love of the sport, that settles in my bones. The random chatter of men already at work, cleaning and maintaining, supporting and overseeing.

I force my eyes open. I take in the bleachers and the boards. The flags and the jerseys. The ice.

My fingers twitch in my gloves as I step onto the smooth ice and push off. Two of the guys from the team are here this morning, but we all give each other ample space. Coach Phillips schedules ice time an hour earlier on Fridays in case anyone wants to get in extra time.

We all know he does it for the mental reprieve it provides. We all take advantage of it when needed.

I settle into an easy skate, warming up slowly.

Nearly a week ago, I stared down a vodka bottle, collapsed in Claire's arms, and promised I'd never hurt her. Already, those promises feel like a noose around my neck. How could I not hurt her?

Every morning, when I leave for practice, she kisses me goodbye and smiles at me like I'm the greatest man she knows. Like I've done something important, saved the polar bears or invented time travel. She cooks dinner each night, keeps our place immaculate, and doesn't complain when my hockey gear stinks up the laundry room.

On Sunday, over waffles and coffee, we had a tough conversation. One that centered on our need to do a better job communicating, being honest, *trusting* each other. It's always been hard for me to talk about my feelings; I hate feeling vulnerable. But with Claire, it's another risk I'm willing to take.

Things with Claire move at warp speed. Within a handful of days, she's settled back in, as if last weekend didn't even happen. But I'm still struggling to process everything, to fully trust this new level of our relationship. As usual, my mental state is dragging behind my physical wants and emotional hopes.

And then, there's dad.

A lump swells in my throat, a bundle of nerves and guilt and...fear.

I grab my stick and a puck and begin a series of stick-handling drills. My mind churns relentlessly but some of my anxiety recedes with a stick in hand.

Three nights ago, Dad called me. When his name appeared on the screen of my phone, my breath froze in my throat and my fingers trembled. Was it Mom? Was there an accident? But the moment I answered and heard his voice, I knew he was drunk. Three sheets to the wind, slurring and swearing. Angry and bitter and jaded.

I clutched the phone tightly and thanked Jesus that Claire was at Rielle's apartment to pick her brain about some marketing ideas.

"You gonna say something?" Dad asked me.

"Are you okay?" I asked slowly.

He guffawed, then hiccupped. "You're just like me, you know."

I bit down so hard, I drew blood, and copper filled my mouth. Like chewing a penny.

"Don't like the truth in that, do ya boy?" Dad asked but it wasn't a question. I fought to control my breathing, to swallow against the anger and ache in my throat.

He laughed, sharp-like. "Who is she?"

"What?" I hissed.

"The woman? You got your priorities fucked up. Your head is all over the place."

"How the hell do you know that? You haven't seen me in over a year."

"Watched your last two games."

At the knowing in his tone, panic rocked through me. Does Dad know it's Claire?

Then, anger. Who does he think he is calling to talk about my play?

Then, insecurity. I played well. Even Coach said so. But could I have been better? Is my head all over the place? Am I not locked in?

Then, anger again. This time, at myself. Why am I letting him get to me? I know he plays head games. So why do I feed into them?

His chuckle, dark and sarcastic, pulls me back to the conversation. "You're still a boy, huh?"

"Why are you calling? Not get your last check?"

His laughter grows and a slickness coats my stomach, making me uneasy.

"Too easy," he wheezes. "Your brother"—he pauses and I clutch the phone tighter—"he took a crack at me. Years ago now but caught me square across the jaw. He told me to leave you the fuck alone. Imagine? He always stuck up for you. Always knew where he stood. Not like you, Easton. You're still so goddamn easy. Rattled by me. By a woman. By a fucking beer."

"What do you want?" I whisper.

"Nothing. Just wanted to see if you were any different after blowing all that money on *help*." He laughs again. "There's no help that can save you, boy. You've got my blood in your veins. Go pour yourself a shot. You've got nothing left. No talent, no credibility, and no fucking balls." His laughter grows and swells, crashing over me like a wave.

For a blink, I'm thirteen again.

My eyebrow is split wide open. Blood streaks down my face, pools in my hands, seeps into the collar of my shirt. It looks worse than it is but it looks bad enough for my head to spin, for floaters to appear in my peripheral vision.

Dad watches me and he fucking laughs.

I swear and take a shot on goal. The puck sails into the net and I breathe out a puff of white smoke.

I glance at the clock. Practice will be starting soon and my head is all over the place. It has been all week. Before I talked to Dad, I was fucked up over Claire. Now, I'm fucked up over everything.

That night, when Claire came home from Rielle's, I confided in her. I told her more about my childhood, my family, my father. It left me feeling unsettled, like I turned myself inside out and all the secrets I keep hidden were on full display.

I'm in too deep. I care about Claire. I love Claire. *Then what the hell is your problem?*

I retrieve the puck and start another drill, skating backwards.

I'm on shifting ground. Everything with Claire feels too big, too raw. Too real.

She's turning my world upside down. She's making me question my future, my plans, my everything. I find myself thinking of ways to make her stay even though she promised she wouldn't go.

And then, I find myself thinking of ways to make her leave because why the hell would she stay?

She's shown you over and over again that she's in this.

Until she's not. I mean, one would think their own parents would stick around, right?

You've got my blood in your veins.

I cut to the side, spraying ice into the air. My breathing is ragged and sweat drips down my forehead. Still, I feel cold.

"Hey!"

I turn at the sound of Noah's voice and watch as my brother makes his way toward me. He skates over to where I'm standing, the smile on his face falling as he takes me in.

"What's going on?" he asks and I don't miss the tremor of worry in his tone. Or the way his eyes scan me over, looking for *signs*.

I hate that everyone looks at me like this. As if they're wondering if I'm even sober, if I care about anything, if I'm really pissed off or blitzed out of my mind. Just like Dad.

I shake my head. "Nothing. I'm good, you?"

Noah frowns. "Try again, East."

The corner of my mouth ticks up at the seriousness of Noah's expression. My whole life, he's the only person I could ever count on. Even now, even though he's moved out and is having a baby, he still tries his best with me.

Even when I don't deserve it. "I was just thinking about Dad."

"Dad?" He rears back.

"And Claire."

His brow furrows. "What do the two of them have in common?"

I think about it and blurt out, "Other than you, they're the only two people I care if I disappoint."

We both blink in surprise. I'm rarely forthcoming and it's even more seldom that I'd be so blunt with the truth. I typically try to share a version of my thoughts without giving them all away.

But right now, I'm confiding in Noah, seeking out my brother's counsel. Because he's the dependable Scotch brother and I still need him.

He watches me closely. "Did something happen?"

"What do you mean?"

"Why are you out here before 6 a.m. thinking of Dad? And Claire?"

I sighed. "Dad called me."

Noah's eyes widen. "Why? I told him to leave you alone."

"You don't have to keep doing that."

"Doing what?" The confusion in his voice is thick.

"Protecting me. You're about to become a father and—"

"I'll always be your brother, Easton."

The quickness with which he responds settles me some and I lean into the reassurance that Noah still has my back. "I'm messed up, Noah."

"What? Now?" He grips my elbow but I shake him off.

"Not like that. I mean, my head is all over the place."

"Stop letting Dad get the best of you."

"And Claire?" I glance up at him, noting the way understanding floods his features.

"You heard about the job." His voice is quiet.

Now, I frown. "What job?"

"Huh? Why else would you be twisted up over Claire?"

I work a swallow. "I'm in love with her."

Noah rears back like I slapped him. "Easton—"

"I'm not joking around. It's for real. I've never felt like this before."

"But your sponsor said—"

"I never would have made it this far without her."

Noah grips my shoulder, his eyes peering into mine. "Fuck," he mutters.

I grin. "Yeah."

"If you guys can manage these past few months, you can manage long distance." He squeezes my shoulder.

I shake my head. "What are you talking about?"

Noah leans back and closes his eyes. He tips his head up and swears again before meeting my gaze. "You don't know. Jesus, East, Claire got a job offer. In New Jersey."

Time stops. For a second, the entire rink looks distorted. My ears clog, as if I've been plunged underwater.

"East?"

Then sound comes roaring back. Suddenly, the ice seems filled with the entire team. Everyone is warming up and I'm huddled in a corner with my brother. We're getting concerned looks and side glances but no one interrupts us.

My head spins and my chest tightens.

"When did you find out?" I murmur, my tone hard. Controlled.

Noah scrapes a hand over his jaw. "Indy told me a few days ago. I thought you knew. I'm sorry, East. I never would have—" He gestures to the rink. "Not now anyway."

I shake my head, shake it all off. All week, I've been struggling to be completely honest with Claire, even when admitting certain truths was painful. She swore she wouldn't leave and yet…she accepted a job in New Jersey and didn't tell me? My hurt is quickly dashed away by anger and I hold onto that. "No, it's okay. I'm glad you told me."

He peers at me. "You sure you're okay?"

I nod and force a grin. "Of course. I'm fine." I tip my head toward the team. "We better go."

Noah gives me a long, searching look.

I shut it down. All the emotions. All the questions. I lock it all down and focus on practice. On hockey. It's the only constant I've ever had and in the midst of losing everything, I won't lose this.

CHAPTER 24
CLAIRE

"I feel like we've turned a corner," I explain to Indy on the phone as I close the dishwasher door and press start. I walk back to the island and pick up my coffee mug. "Things just seem different. Better."

She hums in the background. Her voice is cautious when she says, "That's great, Claire. Really. I just"—big sigh—"are you sure? You guys keep jumping into things. Are you sure you're taking time to process? Is Easton?"

I bite my bottom lip, frustrated by her lack of support. "Indy, I've known Easton for years. Sure, things seemed to go from zero to a hundred but we have so much history."

"But you're not the same people you were five years ago."

I clamp my mouth shut and squeeze the handle of my mug.

Indy's just looking out for you. She doesn't want you to get hurt.

I let out a slow exhale, letting my temper cool.

Why are you so defensive anyway?

"Claire?"

"I'm here."

"I just, I don't want you to get hurt. That's all." She echoes my thoughts.

"I know. It's just, I'm happy. Easton makes me happy. We had a long talk and things are good. Being with him is the only thing I have going for me and it seems like everyone is against it." I plop down on a barstool, frustration causing my emotions to swell. Tears sting my eyes.

"You have a lot going for you, Claire."

I snort.

"You met Big Roxi last weekend."

I grin at the reminder. He already messaged me. Maybe I am being a little dramatic. "True."

"What about the job offer in New Jersey?"

I roll my eyes. "Doing pharmaceutical packaging? Indy, I'll be bored out of my mind. Besides, I don't want to work a traditional nine-to-five. I *like* what I'm doing. I'm making decent money doing it. And I feel like if I keep going, I'll figure it out."

"Have you told Easton?"

"About the job? No. Why would I? When I got the offer, he wasn't speaking to me. And now that we're back together, it seems like an awful time to move. Besides, I don't want the job. If it was my dream job, then yeah, I'd talk to him. But why put more pressure on a relationship that is already fragile for something I don't even want to fight for?"

Indy's quiet for a long moment. "Yeah, that makes sense. I didn't think of it like that."

I'm surprised by the conviction behind her words. She really understands where I'm coming from, which is a relief since my parents sure as hell won't.

"Just, take things slow, Claire. You and East are new. Your new business venture is new. You—"

"Whoa. There's no business venture," I backpedal.

"Why not?"

I sputter, surprised by her challenge. "Are you serious right now?"

"Claire, you're like my sister. I care about you and I want you to be happy. I've watched you try to find your footing since graduation. I had no idea you were so passionate about doing your own thing, and to be honest with you, I think you partly sabotage yourself because you don't want any of the jobs you're applying for. If you did, you'd be on your way to New Jersey. You said if it was your dream job, you would be. What's your dream job?"

I pause, my mug halfway between the island and my mouth. My hand shakes as I give thought to Indy's question. "To create. Design. Be inspired. I just, I want to feel passionate about the work I'm doing."

"And do you? With the band logos and the branding?"

"Yes." My response is a knee-jerk reaction but as soon as I say it, I realize how true it is. My design work fills me with passion and fuels me with purpose.

"Then do it. You should do it."

I grin, placing my mug down and gripping the edge of the countertop. "You really think so?"

"I really do, Claire. If you do some work for Big Roxi, well, you should start thinking of your work as a business. He's going to be big time. And so are you."

I snort.

"If there's anything I can help with, let me know. Reach out to Aiden. But save marketing for Rielle."

I laugh. "Thank you, Indy. Your support really…" I roll my eyes. "God, I hate being mushy. But it means a lot."

"I'm sorry if you felt like you didn't have it sooner."

"Nah, I wasn't as honest with everyone as I should have been."

"As long as you're being honest with yourself, Claire. It doesn't really matter what everyone else thinks or wants."

"True."

"Okay, well, this baby has been pressing on my bladder for the last five minutes of our conversation so—"

"Go pee."

"Call me later?"

"Yeah. Thanks, Indy."

"'Bye Claire."

I hang up the phone and blow out a huge exhale. Easton has been telling me all along to do my own thing. Rielle has helped me brainstorm marketing initiatives. Now, Indy's telling me to go for it. I grin and slip from the barstool. I want to grab my laptop and work out some logo concepts for my brand: ClaireBear Designs.

My foot is on the first step when the front door swings open and Easton steps over the threshold. Immediately, his eyes find mine and, at the anger in his expression, I freeze, my hand gripping the banister.

"Hey. Practice go okay?" Concern spikes in my chest as my mind jumps to worst-case scenarios.

Easton drops his practice bag on the floor and slips off his coat. He drops it on top of his bag and takes two steps in my direction. I falter, stepping down off the step.

"East?"

"When were you going to tell me?"

I cross my arms over my chest, defensive from the accusation in his tone.

"Tell you what?" I ask.

Disbelief ripples over his expression but it's quickly stamped out by anger. His mouth is a thin line, his eyes almost wild with intensity. "New Jersey?"

Damn. I hold up a hand. "It's not what you think."

"How do you know what I think? Have you bothered

to talk to me about it at all?" he snaps, folding his arms across his chest and widening his stance. He looks like the hulk, menacing and furious.

His anger fuels mine and I snap back. "When was I supposed to do that? Last week when I got the offer? Oh wait, you were MIA, hiding out at Panda's place."

He snorts, the sound derisive. "How about Saturday night? When I held you in my arms and made love to you and thought we were building a future."

"We are!"

"Then why didn't you mention it Sunday morning? When we laid everything on the table and swore to be *truthful*."

I wince.

He shakes his head and an expression I can't read blazes across his face. My heart sinks at the betrayal in his eyes. My stomach twists painfully and I press my hands against it. A sharp pang rips through my ribs, and for a second, I wonder if I'm going to fall over.

Concern flares in Easton's eyes but the moment I straighten, it clears. He dips his head and lowers his voice. "I told you I'd always put you first. I swore to you that I'd walk away before I ever did something that would hurt you."

My neck snaps up, confusion blaring in my head. "What are you talking about? How would you hurt me?"

He throws his arms out to his sides, exasperated. "Claire, you can't just give up on yourself because we're together."

"That's not what I'm doing."

"Oh really? Passing up on the stable job with the set salary and the benefits your parents have been gunning for? Cooking dinner every night and cleaning the house in your spare time? Not going out with your girlfriends or hitting the clubs with Rielle?"

"That's not—I'm not—"

"I'm not your pet project," he bellows.

I rear back as if he slapped me. In a way, his words did. Sharp and raw, they scraped over my skin when he hurled them in my direction.

"Easton, I know that. I never tried to change you." My voice cracks and he winces.

"I know that, Claire. You tried to change yourself." His expression is so defeated that I step toward him.

He shakes his head and inches back. The gesture hurts a million times worse than his words, and I wrap my arms around myself, not caring when the tears I've been battling overflow. Two hot tears land on my cheeks and Easton's gaze zeros in on them.

"Easton, please don't do this. Don't do this to me. To us," I whisper, already knowing what he's going to say. And I hate it.

"We can't do this anymore, Claire. You can't settle for less. I won't let you."

"Being with you isn't settling," I sob, desperate for him to see reason. "It's not!"

"And I can't do the highs and lows," he continues as if I never spoke. "It's not good for me, for my recovery."

Well, fuck. That stops me short. I glare at him. "Are you saying that I'm not good for you? That I'm messing with your recovery?" I ask, needing him to say it before I accept it as his truth.

He hesitates and a flicker of hope flares in my chest. But then he schools his features. He meets my gaze head-on. "I'm saying I can't do this with you anymore, Claire. We're not good for each other. You'll end up resenting me and I'll only end up hurting you."

"Like right now?" I gesture toward myself, my face streaming with tears.

Easton doesn't show any remorse as he bites out, "It will only be worse if we had a year invested in this. At least it was only a couple of months."

I shake my head, scrubbing the backs of my knuckles across my face. Still, the tears come. My head spins and nausea rolls through my stomach. He's breaking up with me. He doesn't want me.

I'm not enough for him.

It's a sobering and painful realization.

I nod once, dragging my sleeve across my eyes. "Fine. I'll be out of here tonight."

Easton sighs, as if I'm being dramatic. "Don't be ridiculous, Claire. Take your time. You don't have to—"

"I'm going to pack," I cut him off, whirl on my heel, and clamor up the stairs.

Stepping into his bedroom feels like death by paper cuts. A million tiny lacerations rip at my heart, shredding it. My hands shake and I feel like I'm going to throw up. Still, I force myself to grab anything my eyes land on that's mine. I drop them all into my polka dot duffle bag and stuff my clothes into my small suitcase. It takes less time than it should to pack up my life. In an hour, everything I thought I knew has been dashed to hell and everything I was counting on for my future is nonexistent. I fire off a text message and take one last look around the guest bedroom.

When I drag my suitcase down the steps, Easton strides forward to help me. I hold up a hand, stopping him. "You've done enough for me, thanks."

His expression hardens except for his eyes, which bleed with emotion. But I block them out. He can't have it both ways. Either he wants me or he doesn't. But he doesn't get to cast me aside and then make *me* feel guilty about it.

"Thanks for letting me crash here," I say breezily, pulling my coat from the closet.

"Claire," he sighs. "Where are you going?"

"Home."

"How are you getting there?" Easton stalls, shifting from one foot to the next.

"My ride is out front."

He frowns. "What ride? Who did you call?"

"My brother," I murmur, pulling open the front door. I glance outside and meet Austin's concerned expression at the bottom of the steps.

Austin looks past me and glares. I don't bother turning around to see Easton's face. Mainly because I know it'll hurt and I'm already drowning in pain.

"See ya around, Easton," I say over my shoulder and pull the door closed behind me.

CHAPTER 25
EASTON

The knock on the door has me bolting upright.

It's been four hours since Claire left. Is she back? Part of me hopes yes while the other part prays no.

"I'm really okay. Thanks for hearing me out." I cradle my phone between my shoulder and ear as I stride toward the front door.

"You'll call if you need anything?" my sponsor, Rick, asks.

"Yeah, man. I swear it. I'm straight."

"Okay. Keep your head up, East." He hesitates and I wait for him to continue. "You know, this is why they say not to get romantically involved for at least a year."

"I know," I agree. *But Claire is different, isn't she?*

As soon as I end the call, I pull the door wide open. Noah and Austin stare at me, grim expressions on both of their faces.

"What are you doing here?" I scowl.

My brother gives me a look and pushes past me into the foyer. Austin glares at me for a long moment.

"How is she?" I ask.

He swears and steps inside. I close the door and trail them into the kitchen. Noah fills some glasses of water and reaches into the snack cabinet. He pulls out bags of pretzels and chips.

I lift my eyebrows. "Are we binging tonight?"

"Better than drinking," Austin retorts, his tone sharp.

Noah sighs and points at the barstools. "Both of you, sit. We need to figure this shit out. It's affecting the team, it's affecting your recovery"—he points at me before swinging his gaze to Austin—"and it's affecting your sister."

I wince at the mention of Claire and kind of hate that Noah directed his observation toward Austin and not me. It's not like I don't care about Claire. It's not like I'm not sitting here fucking burning for her.

But how can we move forward if she's not being honest with me? Besides, she deserves more than I can offer, right? The job, the stability, the social life? Did I push her into doing the band stuff? Did my encouragement drive a larger wedge between her and her parents?

A startling thought causes me to freeze. Do Mary and Joe resent me too?

"How is she?" I ask again, desperate for information.

"She's hurt," Austin says carefully. He glares at me. "What the hell happened, man?"

I bite into a chip, relishing the loud crunching sound. We're definitely binging. "She didn't tell me about the job offer in New Jersey. And we got into it."

Austin's eyes narrow. "What job?"

Noah swears. "You didn't know either? What, did she only tell Indy?"

"And probably Savannah and Rielle," Austin admits. He turns his attention to me. "You asked her to stay?"

I rear back. "Of course not. That's why we got into it."

"She wants to turn down the offer." Austin puts two and two together.

"She can't pass up on opportunities because of me," I declare.

"Finally, something we agree on," Austin mutters. I hear the edge of begrudging respect in his tone and I hold on to it.

"Look, Aus, I love your sister."

Austin startles, as if my declaration is the shock of the century. I roll my lips together and consider his expression. Maybe it is. I've never been so adamant about my feelings before, for anyone, never mind a woman. But Claire isn't just some woman; she's mine. Even if she's not with me, I won't ever stop putting her interests ahead of everything else. Ahead of my own wants.

"I want what's best for her," I continue. "And right now, that's not me. Or this." I throw my arms out to encompass the living space Claire and I shared for the past few months. "She should be focused on her career, her life, her friends." I drag my hand through my hair. "Fuck, last week, I took off on her, trying to clear my head. I'm not trying to jerk her around, man." I look at Austin again. "But if I'm being honest, I'm all over the place. I'm not good for her. Not like this."

Austin regards me carefully. Across the island, Noah shifts his weight, crossing and recrossing his arms.

"How are you handling everything?" my brother asks.

"I'm okay. Just hung up with my sponsor when you guys knocked. Honestly, my worst night was last weekend. I came home and there was a bottle of vodka on the counter—"

"What? How?" Noah cuts me off.

I wave a hand, not wanting them to blame Claire but not wanting to lie either. "Claire and Rielle forgot it—"

"Jesus," Austin whispers.

I shake my head. "It's not on her. It's on me. I was crashing at Panda's place anyway. The point is, I'm still battling this. I will for the rest of my life; I know that. But I'm not yet distanced enough from it all to have coping mechanisms. That night, I needed Claire the way I used to need vodka. You think it's fair to place that type of pressure on someone?" I look between Noah and Austin. "Don't get it twisted; I *want* to be with Claire."

Austin stiffens beside me.

"But not if she feels like she can't be honest with me. Not at the expense of her happiness. And not at the expense of making her resent me," I say, leaning back in my chair.

"That's the most grown-up thing I've ever heard you say," Noah comments.

Even Austin nods. "I didn't know it was really like that on your end," he adds after a moment. "My sister, well, apparently she's been twisted up over you for years. I thought you were just…messing around with her."

The fact that he would think that of me, that I'd be careless with his sister, hurts. "I'd never try just casual with Claire. I wouldn't do that to her. Or you or your parents."

"I know that now," he says.

"I've been hung up on Claire for a lot longer than anyone realized." I offer him a smirk. "I'm just better at hiding things."

Austin snorts, shaking his head. "Now what?"

"Now, I focus on hockey. I keep going with my recovery. I learn to move forward. And I give Claire the space she needs to pursue the future she wants."

"That easy, huh?" Noah asks, skeptical.

I shake my head. "It's not easy at all. Letting her go is

the hardest thing I've ever done. But I've been saying it all along; I want what's best for her."

"Me too," Austin agrees.

"Okay." Noah raps his knuckles against the countertop. "So you guys are good?"

I glance at Austin and nod, sticking out my hand.

He slaps it away and throws an arm around my neck, squeezing a little tighter than necessary. "We're good."

"Good," Noah breathes out a sigh.

Austin drops his hold and glances at me and Noah. "Now, let's talk hockey."

I THROW myself into my game.

With the exception of my AA meetings and therapy sessions, I live, breathe, even sleep hockey. In many ways, I feel like a little kid again and it's rejuvenating.

I keep my schedule packed but simple. My routine is intense but welcomed. I focus on repairing my relationships with the guys on the team, especially Austin and Torsten. I pour my all into recovery, attending extra therapy sessions to work through the dark thoughts that still circle in my mind late at night.

It's at one of these sessions that my therapist looks at me thoughtfully and asks, "How often do you still speak with your father?"

I'm quiet as I think about the last year. "When not in rehab," I joke and he cracks a smile, "a few times a month."

"He always calls you?"

I nod. "When he's drunk."

"Why do you answer?"

"Because he's my dad," I respond automatically before leaning back in my chair and letting my answer sink in. "Because I've never not answered."

My therapist nods. "What do you think would happen if you didn't answer?"

Anxiety crawls into my throat the way it always does at the mention of Dad. "I don't know. Maybe he'd call back. Maybe he wouldn't."

"And your brother? What's his relationship with your parents?"

"He stopped interacting with them a long time ago. He sends a check and that's it."

"Do they call him?"

I shake my head. "Not that I know of."

"Do you think a similar arrangement could work for you?" he poses the question gently.

I fidget in my seat, imagining a time when I didn't feel like I was at Dad's beck and call. All those cold nights from my childhood come rushing back. Then, the games he would come watch, banging his fist against the glass to get my attention and hurl out an insult. Followed by the phone calls I've been fielding for the past few years. Every time we hang up, I feel it. The clawing need to drink, the desperation to erase my memories, the desire to be numb. "Maybe," I finally agree.

"Or do you think a possible solution could be to sever the connection on your terms?"

I glance up, narrowing my eyes. "What do you mean?"

My therapist regards me calmly. He's methodical and thorough. Under his scrutiny, I feel like a small child, unable to contain the energy that's buzzing through my veins. Could I do that? Just cut off ties the way Noah did? Why didn't it seem like a possibility before?

My blood is pumping through your veins.

Because I *fear* that I'm like him. That I am him.

"What do you think I mean?" he asks.

I snort. "That I should call up my dad, lay down some boundaries, stick to them, and move forward. Just like Noah did," I blurt out the answer that's been staring me in the face all this time.

"That could be a solution," my therapist agrees without giving anything away.

I roll my eyes and heave out a sigh. "And if he calls again?"

"Do you think he will keep calling after the first few months that you don't answer?"

I shake my head, knowing he wouldn't. Persistence was never his strong suit.

"So?" he prompts.

"So, I could move forward," I realize, running my hand over my jaw.

"It would be a step in that direction."

I mull it over, finally nodding. "It's worth a try."

Dr. Le smiles. "I think so too. Our time for today is up but I'll see you—"

"Friday."

"Friday," he agrees, standing.

I leave Dr. Le's office and consider our conversation all the way to my car. Suddenly, the answer seems so obvious, so easy. I flip on my car and connect the Bluetooth. Then, for the first time in three years, I dial my dad instead of waiting for his dreadful call.

"Yeah," he answers, his voice gruff.

"Dad, it's me."

"What do you want?"

"I want to tell you that I'm done."

He snorts. "What's that supposed to mean, East?"

"I'm done with you," I clarify, my voice steady.

"Now hang on just one minute. Your mother and I can't—"

"You will receive a money transfer the first day of each month. I won't cut Mom off and that means, I'm stuck supporting you too. But that's it. I will no longer pick up your phone calls, whether you're sober or blitzed out of your mind. I will no longer entertain your sob stories or listen to your bullshit and insults. I'm done with you."

He's quiet for a minute and the lack of a response unnerves me.

Then, "Finally wising up, huh?"

"Finally. And I have Noah to thank for it," I say, wanting him to know that I know just how much I owe my brother.

"You have Noah to thank for everything," he barks out.

"Yes," I agree. "And no thanks to you. Take care of yourself, Dad." I hang up.

My hands wrap around the steering wheel and clench tightly. My body feels jittery, with nerves zinging up and down my limbs. I stare out the windshield at the world.

People sipping coffee on street corners waiting for the light to change. Moms hurrying toddlers in snowsuits home from daycare. Cars whizzing by.

I laugh. Oh God, do I laugh. Hysterically, until I'm bent forward, clutching my stomach. It's a huge release, one that lasts for several minutes and leaves me breathless and lightheaded.

My entire perspective shifts in the ten minutes I spend sitting in my car. For the first time, I realize I'll be okay. I won't fall off the wagon again. I have the skills, the will, the purpose to keep moving forward. Just one day at a time, one foot in front of the other. This time, I won't fail.

I drive home, race up to my room, pack my bag, and head to the airport.

I have a hockey game to win, playoffs to look forward to, and a life to start living.

CHAPTER 26
CLAIRE

"Cheers to ClaireBear Designs." Rielle lifts her wine in the air, her eyes glittering.

Indy smiles, clinking her sparkling water with lime against our wine glasses. "Yay!"

I roll my eyes but can't stop the grin that splits my face. "Thank you, girls. I can't believe I'm really doing this."

Rielle waves a hand. "Honestly, it's about time."

Indy nods. "And your parents don't seem too opposed now that you showed them your business and marketing plans."

I wrinkle my nose. "True. But you didn't see Dad's face when I told him I turned down the job offer in New Jersey."

"He sure came around quickly in only three weeks," Indy comments.

"Mom helped," I tell her. When I first told my parents about the job offer in New Jersey, after Austin brought it to their attention, they were elated. I mean, Mom assured me she would miss me if I moved, but they were so proud I landed their dream job for me.

The only problem? It wasn't *my* dream job. I fully came to terms with that when I physically couldn't accept the offer. That, and Big Roxi asked me to design a cover for his next single and some merch mock-ups. He said we're testing the waters and if he likes my product, we can talk about a full album cover. He also signed a letter of engagement with Aiden's firm.

After I turned down New Jersey, I bolted to Rielle's apartment. With her marketing expertise and Indy's flare for research, we drafted a business and marketing plan that had Dad's eyes widening in surprise, Mom's smile stretching across her face, and even Austin's respect.

Within a week, I set up a website, registered an LLC, and began a newsletter. I'm a business owner. Of a small, fledgling, uncertain business but ClaireBear Designs is all mine.

I take a deep sip of my wine, relishing the taste.

"How else are you holding up?" Indy asks me.

I shrug. "I'm okay."

Rielle lifts an eyebrow.

I amend, "I am trying to be okay. I'm hurt. I miss Easton. A lot. But in some ways, I think you guys and even East were right. We jumped into things quickly. It was a lot in a short amount of time and…" I pause, collecting my thoughts. "Maybe I needed this time to sort things out for myself. I feel better now that I have a direction for my life. I love having an outlet for my creativity. If I didn't have ClaireBear Designs, I'd for sure be moping around. I guess I'm just as okay as I can be right now."

"But do you still wish you and Easton were together?" Rielle asks.

I nod. Then sigh. "I don't want to compromise his recovery but when we were together…it was everything at once. You know those love stories you see in movies?

When it's all-encompassing and passionate? Everything with East was like that. There was this intensity, this understanding between us. It was just deeper, more real, than anything I've ever experienced." I offer my cousin and friend a sad smile. "I worry that he's it for me. That I'll never find that with another man again."

I expect them to laugh or brush off my worry. Instead, they both stare at me with concern etched in their expressions. And not the pitying kind of concern but the empathetic kind.

Indy reaches over and takes my fingers in her hand. "It could still happen."

I shrug. "Maybe. How is he?"

Indy heaves out a sigh and Rielle leans forward. Indy glances at us. "You know Noah and I swore we wouldn't get involved in whatever is going on with y'all."

Rielle laughs.

"But, you're my blood, so, he's doing as okay as he can," Indy says.

I frown. "What's that mean?"

"It means he's being like you. He's keeping himself insanely busy. AA meetings, practices, workouts, therapy. He's throwing himself into it with everything he has. But he's also healing, figuring things out, and managing."

"Good." I smile. I mean it too. More than anything, I want Easton to be happy. Even though it hurts that we're not together. Even though he hurt me when we broke up. Even though a lot of things, at the end of the day, I want the best for him the same way he wants the best for me.

If that isn't love, then I don't know what is. But I'm still suffering through love's sacrifices. She really is a fickle bitch.

Indy smiles at me, squeezing my fingers before dropping them. "I'm proud of you, Claire."

I dip into a half bow. "Thank you, thank you. And thank you both for all of your help. I couldn't have pulled it off without you."

Rielle drains her wine glass and grins. "Anytime. I'm just relieved you're not moving to New Jersey."

I laugh. "Yeah, me too."

Rielle stands and nudges the wine bottle closer to me. "I gotta head to work but you stay and drink the wine." She points at me. "You can keep her company." She grins at Indy.

Indy and I laugh but we get to our feet too. "You really have to head to work now?" I ask, knowing the answer.

"You work more than anyone I know," Indy chimes in. "You better get this promotion."

Rielle's smile slips and for a second, a ripple of worry splashes over her face. But then she smooths her expression out and forces a laugh. "Yeah. I hope so."

Something about her voice tugs at me and I touch her arm. "Rielle, is everything okay?" I ask the question that's been circling in my mind for weeks. But for most of them, I was too consumed with my own drama to really ask my best friend how she's managing hers.

Rielle bites her bottom lip and her eyes widen but she nods. "Yeah, I'm okay." She tucks her hair behind her ears and shrugs one shoulder. "I've just been under a lot of pressure at work lately. Sometimes, I feel overwhelmed."

"You sure that's it?" I ask, pressing for more info.

She glances between Indy and me. "I'm sure."

"Okay," Indy says, leaning forward to kiss Rielle's cheek goodbye. "But if you need to vent, you know who to call." She places a hand on her swelling belly. "I pretty much live on my couch after 4 p.m."

Rielle chuckles. "You look amazing, Indy. Glowing and all that."

"And all that," I agree, snorting.

I hug my best friend goodbye and follow my cousin out to her car.

"You think she's telling the truth?" I ask Indy.

Indy unlocks the car doors and pauses with her hand on the handle. "I don't know," she says thoughtfully. "I think she's telling us as much as she can at the moment. She does seem overwhelmed and her job is really intense. She's not an over-sharer so sometimes I wonder if she even knows how to vent."

I nod, agreeing with her assessment. Even though Rielle and I roomed in college, she is a very private person. I pull open the passenger side door. "Want to grab dinner?"

Indy and I both slide inside and she turns on the car. "Mexican?"

"Duh," I agree. Ever since the first time I ate at the Mexican fusion place the day Easton left rehab, I've been a repeat customer. A solid two times a week.

Indy clicks in her seatbelt and backs out of the parking spot, heading toward her apartment. "You going to buy a car now that you're hanging around?"

I laugh, patting the dashboard. "Why would I do that when I have you and Austin to chauffeur me?"

She snorts.

"Maybe," I say slowly. "As soon as I find a place to live."

"Aunt Mary and Uncle Joe already driving you nuts?" Indy glances at me from the corner of her eye.

"They mean well. It's just...I'm ready to move forward with my life, you know?"

Indy nods, stopping at a red light. She turns to me and smiles. "I know. But Claire, you already are."

I think about that the rest of the way to the restaurant.

It sticks with me all through dinner, at night when I stay up late working, and for the rest of the week.

Indy's right. I already am.

TWO WEEKS LATER

The best thing about the start of April? The promise of spring is around the corner. And the Hawks qualify for the playoffs.

The night they win their final qualifying game, the city erupts. Cheers ring out, flags wave from front porches, apartment windows, and cars, and everyone is drinking to a possible Stanley Cup win.

A second-trimester Indy is much more energetic than a first-trimester Indy and we join the excited team at Taps for celebratory drinks.

Tonight, Taps is overflowing with eager fans. The back section of the pub, reserved for the team, is rowdier than usual with players' friends and family members squeezing inside.

Indy's cheeks are bright red from the cold and happiness as she dances next to the bar. Her baby bump is finally noticeable and I'm taking great joy in documenting her pregnancy, much to Noah's delight and Indy's horror. But, as the family graphic designer, we all know who's going to make the elaborate scrapbooks and photo albums. Raises hand.

"Water or ginger ale?" I ask Indy as I lean over the bar to catch Pete's eye.

"Ginger ale," she says.

I nod, glancing down the bar.

Deep blue eyes latch onto mine and I draw in a sharp inhale. Easton's here. His face lights up when he sees me and I work a swallow, drinking him in like it's been years instead of just over a month.

And I want to groan. Out loud for all to hear.

Because Easton Scotch looks incredible. Mouthwatering. Sexy and hot and ripped and—

"Did you order?" Indy elbows me.

I swat her away and continue my unashamed perusal of the only man to make me come on demand.

His shy grin turns cocky the longer I stare but I don't care.

Because his eyes are clear, his skin is brighter, and his mouth. Oh God, that mouth. It's soft and full and I can still recall with perfect clarity the way it felt dragging over my skin.

"Claire?" Indy nudges me again.

Easton slips from his barstool and I don't look away as he makes his way to me.

"Oh," Indy says when she spots him. "I'll be...over there."

I nod, not bothering to look where "there" is.

He moves closer and I turn so my back is pressing into the ledge of the bar. Around me, people call out orders and clamor for Pete's attention. Taps is noisy and crowded. But everything seems to melt away except Easton.

"I didn't know if you'd come," he says when he stops in front of me. Someone knocks into him from behind and he shifts closer, until the tips of our shoes are kissing. "I hoped you would," he admits, gripping the back of his neck and offering me a sheepish grin, "but I didn't know."

"I didn't expect to see you here, either."

He shrugs, glancing around at the team and the crowd.

"It's a big night so… I'm on my best behavior," he jokes, raising a glass with club soda and lemon.

"Congratulations on making the playoffs."

"Thank you."

"You played really well tonight and, well, all month really. You managed to reclaim your spot from Sims."

He nods, slowly. He dips his chin and lowers his mouth to his drink. Easton takes a sip and I stare, mesmerized. "You watched?"

"Every game."

My answer pleases him. His easy grin, the one I remember from years ago, slides across his face. "Now you're just feeding my ego."

I laugh, and a wave of nostalgia pierces my soul. I miss this. With him. I miss him. "Your ego doesn't need feeding."

He shakes his head, winking at me. "Only from you, Clairebear."

I smile, dipping my head. When I look back up, I'm surprised by the seriousness of Easton's expression.

"How are you?" he asks. It's a loaded question and I know by the glint in his eyes that he's asking about everything behind the question.

"I'm okay," I say.

He studies me for a long moment and grins. "Good," he says, satisfied with my answer.

"You?" I ask.

He shrugs. "I'm managing. Taking things day by day. I," he chuckles nervously, scraping a hand over his jaw, "I miss you, Claire. There have been so many times I wanted to reach out and call you. To tell you, God, a million things. Everything."

"I wish you did."

He wets his lips. "Me too." Easton's hand reaches out

and grips my forearm, sliding down slowly until he clasps my wrist. "Can we talk?"

"Sure." *I'd follow you anywhere.* Thank God I don't say the words. Instead, I follow Easton around the side of the bar to a little alcove.

He leans against the wall, his expression intense.

"What's wrong?" I ask, starting to worry that something happened.

He takes a deep breath. "Hear me out?"

I nod.

"I know we haven't talked in a month. I know I have no right to ask you this. But, Claire, my feelings for you haven't changed. If I didn't see you tonight, it would only be a matter of time until I reached out."

I frown, taking his hand in mine and lacing our fingers together. "Easton?"

He smiles that half smile that drives me crazy. "I love you, Claire. God, I'm in love with you. There's, well, there's a lot that's happened. With my Dad. With the team. With my recovery. But I'm doing better. I'm in a better place. And, if you're open to it, and no pressure if you're not—"

"Just say it," I interrupt, losing my patience.

He chuckles and cups the side of my face. "Would you go out with me, Claire? On a real date? And if it goes well and you have fun, would you say yes to a second date? Would you consider long distance? New Jersey isn't *that* far. I can come out for the summer and we can—"

"I'm not moving to New Jersey," I blurt out, frowning that he doesn't already know that.

He pauses, surprise obvious in his expression. "You're not? Why?"

"Because I didn't want the job. I told you that." I grip his wrist that's still holding my face and lean into his touch. I smile at him. "I opened my own business. Claire-Bear Designs. I got a gig with Big Roxi. I'm doing a lot of work for The Burnt Clovers." I wrinkle my nose and lower my voice. "It's going really well."

He closes his eyes and a massive grin stretches across his face. When his eyes pop back open, they're warm with pride. "Really?"

I nod.

"God, baby, I'm so fucking proud of you."

"Thank you," I say. "And I mean that because I don't know if I would have had the courage to start if it wasn't for you."

"You would have," he says with conviction. "Congratulations, Claire."

I bite my bottom lip, staring into his eyes and getting lost like always. I shuffle closer. "But if the offer stands to try for not long distance…"

He drops his head lower and waits for my answer.

"Then I'd say yes."

He smiles, our noses nearly touching. "Yeah?"

I press up on my toes and kiss him. It's slow and soulful. It's better than I remembered. "Yeah."

CHAPTER 27
EASTON

Joe Merrick answers the door and rocks back on his heels. "Come on in, East," he says, stepping to the side.

For the first time in my adult life, I'm nervous entering the Merrick home. "How's it going, Joe?" I ask, slipping out of my coat.

"Fine. You?" He takes my coat and hangs it in the hall closet.

"Pretty good," I say, following him into the kitchen.

"Claire's still getting dressed."

I nod.

"Water or Coke?" He ducks into the refrigerator.

"Coke would be good." I shift my weight from one foot to the other. Joe's been nothing but polite and cordial since he answered the door but that's the issue, he's being polite instead of sincere, stiff instead of warm.

He tosses me a can and rests his lower back against the countertop. The questioning look in his blue eyes, a shade darker than Claire's, is warranted and I sigh.

He deserves an explanation. Jesus, after the way he

tried to guide me after the shit my dad put me through, he deserves a hell of a lot more than my silence. "Joe." I clear my throat, looking him in the eye. I've been through enough therapy to know that stating my intentions from the start is the best way forward. "I'm in love with your daughter."

He straightens at my words, a flicker of surprise but not shock crossing his expression.

"I know I'm not good enough for her," I add. "But I'm trying to be. Claire and I've had a complicated relationship for years. I've tried to stay away from her. I've tried to treat her as Austin's kid sister. I can't do it anymore."

He takes a swig of his Coke, his expression blank.

"I'm sorry for the way I treated her and the way things went down between us. But I want to do this right, the way she deserves. I want to date her. I want her to move back in with me if she wants to. I want to do right by her, by your family. And I'd like for you to be okay with it."

He regards me coolly. "You asking for my permission, East?"

I grip the can of Coke, my heart blaring in my eardrums. Honesty, my old enemy, sounds a gong in my head, a warning and a reminder. "No, Joe." I tell him the truth. "I respect you more than any man I know. But my relationship with Claire is between Claire and me. I'd like your understanding, but I don't need it."

He scoffs, shaking his head. I hold my breath, my stomach knotted. Then, Joe grins and his eyes clear. "You're still as goddamn stubborn as the day I met you."

I manage a half smile, waiting for him to continue.

He laughs now, shaking his head and stepping toward the kitchen island. "I told Mary's dad the same thing."

My mouth drops open. "You did?"

He nods. "My father-in-law wasn't my biggest fan

when I first met him. I was a college dropout without two nickels to rub together."

A college dropout? "I didn't know that."

He waves a hand. "I finished my degree later on. But at the time, I needed the money to help with my mother's medical bills. Jemmy hadn't been called up to the NHL yet. He was still in high school. I don't regret my decision and I'd do it the same way now as I did then. But Mary's dad, understandably, was worried about our relationship. I gave him a line similar to what you said. I'd like your understanding, but I don't need it."

"What'd he say?"

"He laughed, slapped me on the back, and said 'good.'"

"'Good'?"

"Yep," Joe chuckles. "Said no man unwilling to stand up for Mary, even to her own father, was good enough for her. And that's always stuck with me. You've been a part of this family for a long time, East. I know you've had a tough go of things, both as a kid and more recently. I've always believed in your ability to beat anything you put your mind to. I've also known for years that you cared about Claire."

My mouth drops open.

He chuckles, gesturing toward me with his Coke. "Claire hid it a lot worse than you but you have a few tells."

I chuckle.

"Anyway, if I can give you a piece of advice..."

"Please."

"Don't rush it. You went through a lot of transitions this year. So did Claire. They take time to settle. And you guys deserve that time to figure out what you want, both as individuals and, if you decide to, as a couple. Everyone today is always in a rush for the next step. Graduate, work, buy a house, get married, get a dog, have a baby… There's no right process. I was hard on Claire finding a job because I hated seeing her mope around the house without putting her energy into something constructive. I know I wasn't as supportive as I should have been when she came to me with ClaireBear Designs but after seeing how hard she's been working"—he pauses, dipping his head—"and after Mary laid some things out, I can admit that she's doing a really great job. You saw that in her before any of us. You think you're not good enough for Claire because of your past but you're not giving yourself enough credit, Easton. You're not acknowledging how hard you've worked to get to your present. So take your time and have fun dating."

"Daddy!" Claire's voice floats into the kitchen. "Stop reading him the riot act."

Joe snorts. "Stop complaining. Vanny had it worse than you." He winks at me right before Claire enters the kitchen.

I don't respond to Joe because the words are wiped away as soon as I see Claire. Her presence takes the breath from my lungs and rational thought from my mind.

She straightened her hair and it falls to the center of her back. She's rocking some sexy black boots, thick black tights, a distressed denim skirt and an oversized cream sweater. She looks like she just stepped out of a magazine.

But that's not what causes me to smile. I grin because her eyes are shimmering, the apples of her cheeks are pink, and she looks at me like she can't believe I'm here.

Relief blazes through me that this woman, my Claire-bear, is giving me another shot. This time, I won't fuck it up. This time, I vow to take things slow.

This time, I'm not risking it.

"You look beautiful." I place my Coke down.

She blushes and it's the sweetest thing. "Thank you. You clean up all right, too."

Joe and I both laugh as he gestures to the foyer. "Have a good time, kids. Hey, East, I didn't even ask. Where are you taking my daughter?"

I snort, my fingers finding the center of Claire's back. The moment I touch her, I feel more centered. "The Ivy."

Joe whistles. "Pretty fancy for a first date."

"Not when it's this long overdue."

Joe chuckles as Claire and I slip into our winter coats. He opens the front door for us and waves goodbye as we walk down the steps toward my car.

Once we're inside and the heat is blasting, I turn to Claire. "I'm glad you said yes."

She rolls her eyes. "As if any girl would say no to dinner at The Ivy."

I laugh.

"Or to you," she adds.

I reach over the center console and slip my hand into hers. "I love you, Claire."

"Now you're getting ahead of yourself on a first date."

I grin. "You going to give me a hard time all night?"

She shakes her head, smiling as she leans over the console and presses a kiss to my cheek. "Not the whole night."

I squeeze her hand before dropping it so I can pull out of her driveway. Right before I turn onto the street, she says, "And I love you too. I always have."

THE IVY IS a chic restaurant in downtown Boston known for its trendy atmosphere, award-winning menu, and celebrated mixologists. Getting a reservation is like trying to get *Hamilton* tickets—nearly impossible, unless you know who to ask.

Clearly, I called Noah. As always, my brother came through.

Dinner at The Ivy is an experience. But the dessert is on another level.

"Oh my God," Claire moans, biting into the tiramisu. "This is…"

"Heavenly?" I try.

"Orgasmic," she groans.

I snort and she closes her eyes, a smile spreading across her lips.

"I can't believe you ordered the entire dessert menu." Her fork hovers over the raspberry cheesecake.

I shrug, taking a sip of my tea. "I'd be an idiot not to with the sounds you're making."

She blushes but her eyes dance and dazzle. "This is fun."

"Dating?"

"Being with you again. I missed you, East."

"I missed you too, Claire. God, I was such an idiot. I'm sorry, babe, really, truly sorry for the shit I put you through."

She shakes her head, placing her fork down. "No, I kind of understand it. I mean, you totally could have handled it better, but your heart was in the right place."

"I talked to my dad."

"You did?" She leans closer.

"Yeah. I set some boundaries, got some things off my chest. I feel…lighter. Does that make sense? I don't know, Claire. The last year has been challenging as hell. But I feel like it's starting to come together and it's mainly because of you."

"I didn't do anything."

"You did a hell of a lot more than you think." I reach for her hand, gliding my fingertips over her smooth skin. "You woke me up and gave me a purpose."

"Which is?" She lifts an eyebrow, her tone skeptical.

I smile at her. I know she thinks I'm going to say something funny but instead, I give her the truth. "You made me want to be a better man. For you, for me, for us."

"For us," she whispers, her eyes flickering with a hope she's too worried to give into.

I lace our fingers together and give her my truth. Honest, direct, straightforward. "I'm done taking risks, Claire. I want to do this the right way with you."

"What's the right way?"

"Whatever way you want."

She laughs and I grin.

"I want to date you and make love to you and fix your coffee in the morning. I want to support your dreams and see you in my number at my games. I want to live together, in one room, with one bed. You can pick it out."

Her smile widens but her eyes fill with tears. I squeeze her hand and continue, "I want to make a life with you, Claire. But I want to do it right. So it's gotta be at your pace and it has to make sense with the life, the future, you want. What do you think?"

She blinks back the emotion in her eyes as she squeezes my hand back. "I think I want all of that. Everything you just said, I want it. Times a million. Always."

I grin at her and she smiles back and we stare at each other over a table of decadent desserts.

"I have a surprise for you," I whisper.

Panic flares in her gaze. "You're not proposing, right?"

I snort. "Well, if I was, I wouldn't after that expression."

She rolls her eyes. "I just mean, I'm not ready for…"

"I got you, babe. It's not a ring. I think right now, you'll like it even better."

"What is it?"

"It's back at my place."

She gives me a look. "You're not the present, are you?"

I laugh.

"Because that's hardly original, East."

I shake my head. "It's not me either. But thanks for thinking I'm such a great catch. Jesus, I thought you weren't going to give me shit the whole night."

She laughs and drops my hand to scoop up a bite of cheesecake. "Then take me home, East. I want my present. And then, I've got one for you." She waggles her eyebrows.

"Who's being cheesy now?" I ask but I love it.

I love her.

CHAPTER 28
CLAIRE

My mouth drops open. "An office? You made me an office?" I can't help the hushed awe in my voice as I drag my hand over the signage on the guest bedroom door. Except it's not a guest room anymore. ClaireBear Designs, in my brand colors of teal, silver, and white stare back at me. The sign even has my new logo, a small bear with an off-center hat with a star on it. "Oh my God, East."

"Open the door," he says.

I glance at him, suddenly nervous.

He bites his bottom lip and the fact that he seems nervous too gives me the courage to turn the doorknob and step into the room.

I gasp, my breath lodging in my throat. It's beautiful, breathtaking even. White walls with a bold, teal accent wall around the huge window that overlooks the street. A gorgeous oak desk with a white and light gray chair. Silver wire baskets and a desk set sit atop the desk, already filed with office essentials. An iMac sits in the center of the desk, causing my eyes to nearly fall out of my head.

I stand in the center of the room and slowly spin around. Each detail that my gaze catches on causes the lump in my throat to swell larger. There's even art. Three pieces of mixed media that depict Boston's musical legends, local venues, and popular city details hang along one wall while the other showcases built-in bookshelves. There's a set of geode agate bookends that look awfully familiar. I step closer to them, grinning when I realize they're from my bedroom at my parents'.

I glance at East. "How did you..."

"Indy," he explains. He shuffles back on his heels, his hands stuffed in his pockets.

I close the distance between us and throw my arms over his shoulders. "Thank you. Thank you so much, Easton. This is, God, it's beautiful. I can't believe you, I mean, how did you even..." I blow out a breath and kiss him hard. When I pull back, I'm pleased to see the happiness that rings his irises.

"You really like it?"

"I really love it."

He breathes out a sigh of relief. "Good. I'm glad."

"How did you pull this all together?" I ask, spinning around again.

"I had some help." He laughs. "One of my teammates from college, his wife Charlie is an interior designer. She's pretty big time in New York City now, but when I explained this project, she leapt at the chance to help out. Indy's recruited her to do the baby's nursery. I have her contact info if you want to change anything."

I shake my head. "No way. This is perfection."

"Good." He drapes his arm over my shoulders and pulls me into his side. "Then it's yours."

"So, I'll be going to the office now?" I ask, glancing up at him.

The color in his face heightens and I hold back my laughter. Easton Scotch is blushing!

"I don't want to rush anything, Claire. Your dad gave me some good advice—"

I groan and he chuckles.

"But whenever you're ready, I'd love for you to move back in. In the meantime, yes, consider it like you're going to the office. We even have coffee."

I laugh and snuggle deeper into his side. "Thank God because Mom is driving me insane."

He glances down at me, his eyes bright with humor. "Mary? No."

We both laugh and I turn into his embrace.

Easton threads his fingers together at the base of my spine and pulls me closer. Reaching up onto my tippy toes, I raise my mouth to his. When he kisses me, the entire world melts away and it's just us again.

Easton kisses me with promise and I kiss him back with my unwavering certainty. This time, I know we're going to be okay. This time, I truly believe we are meant to be.

In every fiber of my being and in the deepest part of my soul, I know that Easton is mine the same way I am his.

And the second the playoffs are over, I fully intend to move in.

His lips drag over my cheek, down the column of my neck. I arch into him as his hands drop, squeezing my ass.

I giggle and pull Easton down to the floor with me. The fluffy white rug cushions my head as his body shadows mine. Easton pulls back and grins at me as I unbutton the line of buttons on his dress shirt. Then, he drops his head again and kisses me slowly.

We christen my office before moving on to the other rooms in the house.

And it's perfect. Perfectly us.

EPILOGUE

TORSTEN

Taps is quieter than usual tonight. Maybe it's because I'm here earlier? I glance at my watch. It's 9PM.

Maybe it's because Tuesdays are slower? Nah, that's not it.

Maybe it's because you're realizing just how alone you are?

The thought rips through me and I gesture to Pete, the bartender, that I'm ready for a shot. Last week, my hockey team, the Boston Hawks, qualified for the playoffs. I was riding a natural high, filled with excitement and pride. I was so thrilled, it was easy to block out the increasing pressure around my knee when I push onto the ice. I was even able to ignore the tightness in my shoulder that extends to my chest when I'm aggressively stickhandling.

But then yesterday happened.

Yesterday, I sat down with Hawks owner, Scott Reland, Coach Phillips, and senior management. I had the toughest conversation of my career, of my life, and it ripped me wide open. But, the truth will do that to you.

I had to admit that my body is broken. That I'm not recovering from the hits and the surgeries and the layering scar tissue the way I did a decade, hell, even five years ago.

As much as I wish it wasn't true, it's time for me to hang up my skates. A bittersweet taste, more bitter than sweet, fills my mouth and I pick up my beer and take a swig. I can't imagine my life without hockey. It's been the one constant I've clung to since I was a nineteen-year-old kid. The one thing I could count on, save for Farmor, my grandmother. But she's in Norway and I'm here and...

Unless I can find a way to stay in Boston, I'll be forced to leave the US when my contract expires at the end of June. I rub my palm over my chest. That's the real issue, isn't it?

I toss back the tequila and let its warmth unfurl through my body.

Of course losing hockey hurts. But losing my home, the life I built, the only life I truly know, aches right on top of it.

I manage to grin at some guys who sit a few seats over at the bar, shooting me glances.

I've been in Boston for so long, a part of the Hawks franchise for so many years, that even fans forget that I'm not from here. Can I really move back to Oslo now? After all this time? With so many irreparable wounds between Father and me? Between my brother Anders and me?

"Hey Pete," I call out. When he looks up, I tilt my head. "I'll take another shot, please."

"You got it, Hansen. We're all pumped that you're heading to the playoffs." He pours the tequila and places it in front of me.

My stomach knots and my chest tightens. I force a smile. "Thanks, man. I can't wait."

A group of women, three friends, mid-twenties, enter Taps. The little bell jingles over their heads and they giggle. They're beautiful, every single one of them, and I take a moment to study them.

When the brunette looks up, her eyes catch mine, and her gaze lingers for a beat too long. The invitation in her glance is clear as day and I chuckle, tipping my shot glass in her direction before taking it.

I wish I had a woman to go home to. I wish I didn't have to make all of these decisions on my own. But I've been on my own for a long time now.

Last night, my lawyer Bill joked that the easiest, fastest way to stay in the States would be to get married. *Married.*

The longer I sit at the bar, the more an idea grows in my mind. An idea I shouldn't even consider. But here I am, turning it over like it's a viable option.

I've been a perpetual bachelor for so long, I don't know the first thing about being in a serious relationship. I definitely know nothing about *marriage.*

But I do know a lot about commitment and communication and living up to my word.

I frown. This is crazy, right?

Who would even want to marry me?

Black hair, dark, mysterious eyes, and a rosebud mouth flash in my mind. Curves that make my mouth water and hair I want to tangle my fingers in, knot around my knuckles. I shake my head, pushing the images from last month away. All I did was make sure a drunk girl, my captain's little sister's best friend, got home okay. Nothing happened between us save for some innocent flirtation.

Nothing that would lead me to think of her like *this.* Now.

Still, my eyes are pulled back to the women at the end of the bar. They're laughing and talking, their hands gesturing, their wine glasses dangling from their fingers.

What if I had a woman, a partner, to share my life

with? What if I had someone who loved me, a wife to go home to?

What if I could find a real reason to stay?

DO you love marriage of convenience romances? How about billionaire heartthrobs? If yes, then you don't want to miss Torsten and Rielle's story! It's hot and sweet and overflowing with feels! Start reading *The Faker* now!

ALSO BY GINA AZZI

Knoxville Coyotes Football:

Faked and Fumbled

Surprised and Sacked

Trapped and Tackled

The Burnt Clovers Trilogy:

Rebellious Rockstar

Resentful Rockstar

Restless Rockstar

Tennessee Thunderbolts:

Hot Shot's Mistake

Brawler's Weakness

Rookie's Regret

Playboy's Reward

Hero's Risk

Bad Boy's Downfall

Lock 'Em Down

Boston Hawks Hockey:

The Sweet Talker

The Risk Taker

The Faker

The Rule Maker

The Defender

The Heart Chaser

The Trailblazer

The Hustler

The Score Keeper

Second Chance Chicago Series:

Broken Lies

Twisted Truths

Saving My Soul

Healing My Heart

The Kane Brothers Series:

Rescuing Broken (Jax's Story)

Recovering Beauty (Carter's Story)

Reclaiming Brave (Denver's Story)

My Christmas Wish

(A Kane Family Christmas

+ *One Last Chance* FREE prequel)

Finding Love in Scotland Series:

My Christmas Wish

(A Kane Family Christmas

+ *One Last Chance* FREE prequel)

One Last Chance (Daisy and Finn)

This Time Around (Aaron and Everly)

One Great Love

The College Pact Series:

The Last First Game (Lila's Story)

Kiss Me Goodnight in Rome (Mia's Story)

All the While (Maura's Story)

Me + You (Emma's Story)

Standalone

Corner of Ocean and Bay